To H.

CW01402597

MANDy

STEPHANIE SPARKS

Make good choices...

Stephanie
Sparks ♡

Content Warning

Mandy contains subject matter and themes related to necrophilia, body horror, kidnapping, car accidents, consent, violence and sexual violence, and death.

Reader discretion is advised.

For the weird girls

MANDY

No good deed goes unpunished.

— *Unknown*

CHAPTER I

The last thing Mandy Fisher expected to hear in the dead of night was a fist banging on the door. It woke her like a thunderclap. Unexpected, jarring. She slowly sat up, holding her covers close to her chest. She listened, but couldn't hear beyond the blood rushing to her head, outside of which there was only silence. And the knocking.

When the frantic pounding began again, it wasn't a dream or her imagination playing tricks. She was all alone in her father's house on an acreage that was a two-hour hike to the nearest town. Visitors in the middle of the night were rare, even in her father's line of work.

She laid back down, pulling the blankets over her head. She couldn't fall asleep, nor could she make the knocking stop. It became louder, more urgent, and then a voice cried out.

"Help us!"

Us. Meaning more than one.

Meaning Mandy would be outnumbered.

"Go away," she whispered, breath hot under the covers.

But they wouldn't go away. The back porchlight was on. She had forgotten to turn it off and so it became a beacon for her midnight guests.

The stranger called out again. "I know you're in there!"

She pushed the covers aside, easing off the bed. Her feet touched the cold, hardwood floor. The planks creaked. She bit her lip as if to quiet her movements, as if the panicked stranger down below could sense her exact location.

He knew someone was in the house and he wasn't going to stop banging on the door until either she answered it or he had smashed his way inside.

"Help us, please!"

Mandy grabbed her robe from the hook on the door. She wrapped it around herself, cinching the belt tight. Against her better judgment, she kept the lights off so that under the cover of darkness she could see who was at the door, get a description, and report them if necessary.

Not that she had anything against visitors, but something about strangers in the dark turned her stomach to ice. She never cared much for the company of others — with one exception, but he was long gone.

And he was definitely not coming back.

She tiptoed down the stairs, keeping her back against the wall but also careful not to brush against the family photos trailing downward. Her father and mother on their wedding day in a tiny church. A family photo of the three of them, Mandy just barely able to hold her own head up on her wobbly infant neck. A photo taken before cancer claimed her mother's life. Kindergarten, grade school, junior high pics. Braces clamped on tight and shining in one awkward school photo.

Her graduation photo's frame hung in the exact spot it had been placed years ago; the photo conspicuously absent. Her father hung it in earnest, but after everything that happened that spring, the last thing on his mind would have been to take the frame down.

Mandy gripped the tie around her waist as she approached the front door. She could see through the glass arch out onto the porch, but that light was off and no one was there. She waited for a bloodied hand to slap against the window, like in the movies she was advised to avoid, lest they aggravate her condition.

Mandy rounded the stairs. She passed by the sitting room where her father kept stacks of books and magazines. Then the formal dining room where he handled the bulk of his paperwork. Then the kitchen where he thankfully did not conduct any of his work.

No, that had been Mandy's mistake.

Her crime scene.

At the end of the hallway was a half-lite door, and just before the door, if Mandy turned left, was the entrance to her father's business. It was where the Fisher house became the Fisher & Sons Funeral Home.

There were no sons, however. Just Mandy and her father, and the occasional hired hand when business picked up. Her father thought the "sons" made the name sound homey and personal.

While Mandy was quite satisfied with being an only child, tonight she wished she had some big, strong brothers to protect her because she could see the stranger at the backdoor. His chin dropped onto his chest as he rested his head against the glass. He was young. Maybe Mandy's age. It was hard to tell in the dark, the porchlight casting harsh shadows across his brawny features. His hair fell in a sweaty mess across his cro magnon forehead and heavy brows. A gash above his hairline oozed blood. His nose was busted and bloody. He was a thick boy — a man built for tackling, running, crushing, destroying. If he wanted to, he could make short work of the tired door. But he didn't. Not yet. He was at least that little bit civilized.

All Mandy had to do was stay out of sight. Eventually he would have to go away. She was about to go back to bed. Her slight movement caught his attention. The second he glimpsed her, peeking down the hallway, his eyes widened and he started knocking all over again.

"Oh, shit, hey! You gotta help! My friend— There was an accident. I don't know what to do."

Mandy knew what to do.

Don't let them in.

Go back to bed.

Forget this ever happened.

Her father's words made her pause and reconsider. In the two years she spent in the rest home, he never once brought up the incident that put her there or forced any fatherly wisdom upon her. Not until the hot summer day he arrived to take her home. Then he let it all out.

"Make good choices, Mandy, and be kind to others," he said, wiping the perspiration off his ruddy face. As usual for a workday, he wore a full suit and tie. The heat was cruel to his jolly body, but never affected his friendly disposition. "You're an adult now, so more than ever, you're responsible for what happens to you. It's easy to wall yourself off from others and keep your head down, but you can still do good in this world. You just have to make the right choices."

In the car on that long drive home, Mandy stared out the window and listened to her father's sermon. She didn't know if he meant what he was saying or if he was just trying to fill the silence, but his words stuck with her.

And he was right. All she wanted to do was shut out the world and try to move on with her life. The problem was she worked for her father, and his business was a people-facing, customer service one. It would reflect terribly on the business if she ignored a stranger's pleas for help, only for her father to come home and find him, and then do what she should have done in the first place: Help him.

Make good choices. Be kind to others.

She sighed, dislodging her teeth from her bottom lip. Coming out from the darkness, she went to the door.

The stranger pawed the glass, like a sad, desperate puppy.

"Please."

Mandy turned the lock. The brass slipped between her fingers as the stranger shoved his way in, invading her space. He reeked of blood, sweat, musky cologne, and beer. He loomed over, breathing hard.

Just as quickly, he moved aside and pointed outside to a crumpled mess at the bottom of the steps. A young man's unmoving body.

"You gotta do something."

CHAPTER 2

What could she do? He was dead. Mandy had worked with enough dead bodies to be certain without checking his vital signs. The stranger picked him up and carried him inside, and Mandy led him into the funeral home side of the house. They passed through the reception area like ghosts, gliding over the maroon rug and breezing past the dried flowers in ornate vases.

Mandy turned on as few lights as possible. She didn't want to light up the whole house and give the neighbors — even though they were acres away — something to talk about.

Gossip — that's what the Pomerleaus would do. The neighbors and people in town liked to talk about Mandy and the horrible thing she did. She was never going to forget and neither would they.

"What's your name?" she asked the stranger so he wouldn't be so strange anymore.

"Chaz. Charles to my folks, but everybody calls me Chaz." He said it on autopilot, as though it were a line he gave every time he introduced himself, no matter how bleak the situation. "Is he going to be okay?"

Mandy couldn't tell if Chaz was dumb or in denial. She guided him into the embalming room and instructed him to lay his friend out on the dressing table. It was more respectful than leaving him on the floor.

"Now what?" Chaz asked.

"Umm..." Mandy looked around. They could call the police. That was exactly what her father would do. A white, slimline phone hung on the wall, cord dangling down. "We should call the police."

"What?" The word blew out of his mouth, beer fumes assaulting her nostrils. "No, no, you can't do that. Just fix him and we'll go."

Fix him? "What do you think this place is?"

He whirled around. A tornado whipping open drawers and bumping the stainless steel table. He found some of her father's tools.

"You do medical shit, don't you?" His pitch startled Mandy. "Just do something!"

"I'm not a doctor," she said, making a break for the phone. "I think we should call the police."

As she lifted the phone from its cradle, Chaz ripped it out of her hand and slammed it back down.

"Jesus Christ! No goddamn police! We were drinking, okay? They're gonna lock us up and throw away the key."

They would lock *Chaz* up for whatever drunk driving accident had caused the death of his friend. His friend would be buried or cremated, and wouldn't have anything to worry about.

Unable to face the violent, sulking stranger, Mandy turned her attention to the young man on the table. He was pale and slender, much smaller than his hulking companion. His neck was broken, of that Mandy was certain, but his face had not a scratch. His wavy blonde hair, though a bit disheveled, appeared like a golden halo. He was an angel.

She touched his face, hoping he was still alive. But he already felt much too cool.

"I'm sorry," she said softly, not looking at Chaz.

"Sorry for what?" When she didn't answer, he pounded a fist on the counter. *"Sorry for what?!"*

"He's dead," she said.

"No..." he wailed, grabbing his head as if it had been split open. He dropped onto his knees and began to sob. "Why? Oh, god, why?"

Mandy crossed her arms, remembering that she was in her robe and nightgown. Her feet were crammed in a pair of ratty slippers. How she appeared was the last thing on Chaz's mind, but her skin still crawled. She wanted him to leave. She wanted to be able to call the police. What did he think was going to happen, that she would bury the young man without any fuss? Make all his problems go away?

She shuffle-stepped to the door, hoping he would take notice and be on his way. She rubbed her arms, wondering how she was going to explain the dead man to her father. But as she passed by the dressing table, her fingers traced the stainless steel and she gazed again at the young man's angelic face.

Chaz sniffled and snorted into the crook of his elbow. "Robbie was, like, the best guy ever. He was always there for his friends. He just wanted to look after me. I was too drunk and he tried—" Body-wracking sobs cut him off and he curled up in the corner.

Mandy leaned slightly over him. *Robbie.* That was a name she didn't hear too often. Robert and Rob were still quite common in town, but *Robbie?* There was something charming in a name that seemed to be from a different time. Like her own name — mocked for a cheesy '70s song that was allegedly inspired by the songwriter's dog. When the boys in junior high learned that little tidbit, they mocked her relentlessly.

But not Trevor.

Her heart ached. Robbie's perfect skin reminded her of Trevor, another dead boy. She stroked his cheek. Her eyes darted toward Chaz's corner, but he hadn't seen her do it, too blinded by his own grief.

Trevor shouldn't have died so young either. It was unfair.

Her fingers grazed Robbie's hair. Nothing too incriminating, but her skin burned when Chaz lowered his hands and cried, *"Isn't there anything you can do?"*

Standing rigidly, Mandy stepped away from the table. Away from Robbie. She was afraid. Not because of her proximity to a dead body, but because of her own touch. She still didn't understand her gift.

It's not a gift. It's a trick.

It's a curse.

But to rid her house of these two strangers, perhaps — just for tonight — it really was a gift.

CHAPTER 3

TWO YEARS EARLIER...

M abel Marie Truscott died on Christmas Day. She had a belly full of food after squeezing in three family visits where she was plied with cinnamon buns and coffee, cookies, treats, two turkey dinners, and assorted deli platters. Mabel was never one to turn down a free meal — she was living on a fixed income in her golden years — or an opportunity to pinch the rosy cheeks of her many grandchildren.

After refusing all offers for a ride home, she hoofed her way back to her apartment through the thick snow. Halfway there, she realized she had forgotten her keys at someone's house. Like the funds in her savings account, her memory was slipping away a little more each day, so she couldn't recall at whose house.

But rather than turn around, she forged ahead and arrived at her building. She must have hoped some other resident would buzz her in, and perhaps it was for the best that no one did, because as soon as she scraped her boots on the welcome mat, her

86-year-old heart gave out on her and she collapsed at the front door where the landlord soon found her.

A week later, just after New Year's Day, Mabel was wrapped up in her Sunday best and laid out in an affordably nice casket. Mandy spent the morning applying makeup to the old woman's face to give her a bit of life.

Once Mabel was taken care of, Mandy had to rush around, placing program booklets on each seat in the chapel. From there, she borrowed her father's van to pick up the wreaths at the floral shop downtown.

In her rush to get back to the chapel (ever mindful of her father's voice that nothing was more important than the day of the funeral service), Mandy hit a patch of ice. The van slid right toward the end of the funeral procession. She slowed down just in time to ever-so-gently bump the black pickup truck parked at the end.

Gripping the steering wheel, she stared in shock as the driver of the truck threw open his door and swung a long leg out. He was dressed all in black — black cowboy boots, black jeans, black blazer over a black button-down shirt, and a black cowboy hat on top. Under all that black was Trevor Hardisty.

Mandy was terrified. She knew Trevor from school — *everyone* knew Trevor. He was the star football player. He was going to go far. He already had several scholarships lined up because he could run with a ball from one end of a field to the other. Mandy didn't get what was so special about him or the sport he was so good at, but she never yucked anyone's yum. They were from different worlds, and now those two worlds had literally collided.

Grim lines etched into his young face, Trevor approached the van. She jumped out of her skin when he tapped his knuckles on the window. She rolled it down a tiny bit, expecting to be hosed with vitriol and offensive language or pure, blinding rage.

Instead, Trevor leaned in and looked right at her. "Are you okay? Are you hurt?"

She was not, just shaken. She had never been in an accident before.

Trevor helped her out of the van and she stood in the bitter cold, snow creeping into her boots, to look at the damage to both their vehicles. His truck had a broken taillight and a white scratch from the van's paint. She stammered an apology and a promise to exchange insurance with him, but he laughed and rubbed his elbow over the bumper.

"Naw, it'll buff right out," he said. "Don't worry about it. Hey, don't we go to the same school? I thought I'd seen you somewhere before."

Mandy was not someone people recognized anywhere. She scurried through life as silently as a mouse, fearing her mere presence was a blight on an otherwise rodent-free world. But if someone like Trevor noticed, then maybe more people were aware of her.

She wasn't sure how to feel about that.

Time was ticking. The service was about to begin. Trevor insisted on helping her carry the flowers into the chapel. As he and Mandy rushed around to set them up, he brushed off confused queries from the funeral-goers, like *What are you doing? Where are you going?*

"Everyone seems to know you," she observed quietly as they put the finishing touches on Mabel's casket.

He smiled sadly, glancing at the old woman in the box. "Oh, you know, it's my grandma's funeral."

Surprised, Mandy never got to give her condolences or thank him for his help before he joined the rest of the funeral-goers, slipping in between a few other folks dressed in black. Even as he removed his hat and settled in, Trevor stood out. She couldn't take her eyes off of him. He gave her a wink.

After the service, as people drifted out of the chapel and to their cars for the reception at someone's house, Trevor lingered at the exit. Mandy was hurrying to tidy up and help her father, but she took a moment to summon her courage and walk up to him. She tapped him on the shoulder and before she could say thanks, he smiled at her.

"You again."

Embarrassment burned her face. She regretted approaching him. Girls like her weren't supposed to talk to guys like him. She wasn't anyone special on a regular day, and today, she was less than trash because it was his grandmother's funeral and she had bashed into his truck.

She shook her head, backing away. "I'm so sorry," she mumbled. "For everything."

"That's okay," he said. "Hey, do you need any help?"

"No."

"I'd love to help. I hate standing around feeling useless. Grandma's gone and me dwelling on it is not gonna make anyone feel any better." He followed Mandy back into the chapel where she tried to move him along, insisting that she could handle everything just fine. But he took her hand, squeezing it. "Please. Let me do something. Talking to you will keep my mind off everything. And besides—" He pointed at the wreath. "—I'm great with flowers."

She smiled nervously, and for the next hour, they collected all the flowers and discarded program sheets. They tidied up the pews and found a few lost scarves and mittens that had been left behind. He made a joke about getting hired at the funeral home so they could work together again, and as much as that joke unsettled her, she also secretly liked the idea of being around him again.

Nothing lasts forever, and soon Trevor had to go home.

But that wasn't the last of him.

He called her house. He left her notes at school when the winter semester started. He smiled at her in class and when he passed by in the hallway. On Valentine's Day, he slipped a daisy into her locker, and later that night, while her father dozed off in front of the TV, he showed up at her door with a box of chocolates. Bundled up against the February cold, they sat on the porch and polished off the box together.

"Why do you keep coming around?" she asked.

He cocked his head to one side, considering her question. "This is the first time I've ever been to your house."

"You know what I mean."

He smiled. "I don't know. I guess I just kinda like talking to you. You're different from the other people at school."

"You don't think I'm kinda weird?"

"We're all kinda weird."

"You're not."

"I'm weird about football, I guess."

"That's not weird."

"It is if you play it so much that people give you scholarships to do it and you gotta ice your elbow after every game."

"I guess..."

"We've all got some weird trick we can do," he said, gazing at her with his warm brown eyes. He reached out, wiping chocolate from the corner of her mouth. The stroke of his thumb against her lips took her breath away. Then he popped it in his mouth and sucked the chocolate off. "Mine's football. What's yours?"

Mandy wouldn't find out until spring.

CHAPTER 4

M andy never forgot that Mabel Truscott was the reason why Trevor started hanging around. She thought about the woman often. The first time he kissed her was because he followed her along to prepare for a graveside service. He disappeared for a few minutes to leave flowers on his grandmother's grave and then raced right back to Mandy's side.

She commented on his devotion to the old woman and he blushed. Then when she turned her attention back to her work, he leaned in and gave her a peck on the lips. She stared at him in stunned silence, willing him to go away while also praying he would try it again.

He took her hand instead and led her on a walk through the melting slush of the cemetery. It was mid-March at this point. He sat her down on Mabel's headstone, and though Mandy had no preconceptions about the afterlife, she still felt badly about trodding on the woman's grave.

"So what do you think about going to prom?" Trevor asked, clearing snow away from Mabel's flowers with the toe of his boot.

Mandy shrugged. "It's a dance. I don't like to dance."

"You don't have to."

"And I don't have money for fancy clothes."

"Wear whatever you like."

She looked him in the eye and responded honestly. "There's going to be lots of people. I don't like people."

Trevor grinned. "You like me."

Mandy blanched. She did like him, but he wasn't supposed to know, or at least know it was so obvious. She liked him with the caveat that he would eventually abandon her to chase after a much prettier girl. Mandy wasn't his type and she wasn't going to fool herself into thinking she ever could be.

When Mandy didn't say anything, he slipped his hands around her. "What do you say? Go to the prom with me?"

Mandy had seen this movie before. She goes to the prom with the most popular guy in school and her classmates and teachers were all going to laugh at her. Maybe this was a prank. Maybe he wanted to make her look like an idiot. If so, she didn't have telekinetic powers to teach them a lesson.

"I don't think that's a good idea," she said meekly, slipping out of his embrace.

Instead of storming off or causing a scene, he laughed. "Oh, I get it. You think I'm messing with you."

"No..."

"Yeah, you do. Come on, I'm not gonna pour blood on you, if that's what you think."

"I wasn't thinking that," she lied. "I just don't think we're a good match."

He knelt in front of her, knees sinking into the wet earth and sludgy snow. He grasped her hands in a formal proposal pose. "I really like you, okay? Prom is important to me and I kinda think you are too. Believe me..." He looked around at their surroundings. "You're the only girl I've ever followed into a cemetery. I think you're special."

"You're teasing me." She tried to pull away, but he wouldn't let go.

This time he wasn't smiling. He was dead serious. "I like you, Mandy. Let me take you to prom."

How could she say no?

When she told her father about their plans, he jumped out of his easy chair and danced her around the room. He gave her his credit card and begged her to buy a dress and offered to take her shopping in the city. Mandy took his card, but spent her own money on the dress, a simple blue number she found at the second-hand store in town.

Through the rest of March and April, Trevor kept coming around. Sometimes, when the weather was warm enough, they would sit on the porch and drink tea, or they would walk the perimeter of the acreage, or he would drive her around and they would talk until her curfew. And each time he dropped her off, he held her a little longer, until one time she tilted her head to look at him and her lips accidentally brushed against his jaw.

He smiled. "If you wanted to kiss me so bad, all you had to do was ask."

"No, that's not—" But instead of lying and making excuses, she shut up and kissed him.

Parked outside her house, they kissed for an hour. Emboldened, she curled a hand around the back of his neck and sank down in her seat until he was almost on top of her.

Their relationship escalated from there. They kept their hands to themselves at school because Mandy was uncomfortable with attention and didn't care to infiltrate Trevor's inner circle of school friends.

But at night after the sun went down, they would park on the farthest edges of civilization and go to town on each other. Mandy had just about explored every inch of Trevor's body when they climbed into the back of his truck under piles and piles of blankets one late April night. Under the blankets, they kept each other warm and had sex for the first time.

"So... What did you think?" Trevor asked after a few quiet moments of cuddling.

Mandy, who had come into the situation with no expectations other than that the first time was not supposed to be that great, found that the opposite was true. It had been amazing. She smiled back at Trevor, squeezing the arm he wrapped around her.

"Not bad," she said.

A few weeks later, prom came and went uneventfully — no cruel classmates, no buckets of blood, no tragedies.

Well, except for one — because this is not a love story.

As uneventful as the prom was, the after-grad party promised to be anything but. Mandy resisted going. She hadn't packed a change of clothes or had any intention of following Trevor and his rowdy friends out to one's farm for a night of drinking. They had been polite enough to her during the dinner and dance, which had been attended by family members and teachers, but the after-grad party was when the graduates let their hair down. Mandy was uncertain how nice they would be when parents and teachers weren't around to make sure everyone was on their "best behavior."

But Trevor pleaded. "Come on, it's time you met the crew. They're my best friends and they're gonna love you because *I* love you."

"You love me?"

"You know I do," he said.

He ran his fingers through her hair. A cool breeze blew through the parking lot of the community hall where the prom was hosted. The other grads were forming groups and jumping into each other's cars, shouting assorted directions to the farm they were going to meet up at. Noise and confusion from the revelry was enough for Mandy to put her trust in Trevor.

They kissed. A truck sped by blasting country music. One of their classmates hung out the passenger side window, pointing and laughing at them. The night only got worse from there.

The farm was hardly a farm — a worn-down barn surrounded by rusted machinery and dead cars. The ground was swampy from the winter meltoff. Mandy hitched up her dress to keep the hem from getting soiled — and then her shoes got stuck. Trevor carried her the rest of the way.

When they finally got to the barn, any plans for having an intimate moment together flew out the window.

Trevor's football buddies roped him into a drinking game. One of them performed a keg stand, another shotgunned a beer, while a third laughed like a braying mule. Suds sprayed across Mandy's dress, while their girlfriends tsked and said what a shame. They had changed into jeans and sweatshirts back at the venue, and didn't hesitate to let Mandy know that this party wasn't their first after-grad rodeo. In a small-town graduating class of sixty-something seniors, Mandy was surprised at how few of them she actually knew. One of the girlfriends even asked if she was from another school.

"No, dumbass," admonished her friend. "That's the funeral home girl."

"Oh..."

Mandy shrank down, wishing Trevor would take her home, but she had lost track of where he had gone. Finally, unable to sit around waiting for the hours to crawl by, she hitched up her dress yet again and wandered around, looking for him.

He stood among a group of friends gathered around a garbage can fire. They were laughing and joking. Trevor wiped a tear from his eye and then he smiled at Mandy.

"Hey."

"Can you take me home?" she asked.

"Why? What's wrong?"

"I want to go home," she replied sternly.

"Uh-oh, Trev," chided one of his pals. "Trouble in paradise!"

The others howled like hyenas. Mandy ignored them, but Trevor could not. As she whispered to him how badly she wanted to leave, the "friends" roasted the couple. Trevor led Mandy away — and just when he thought they were out of earshot from their awful, humiliating comments, someone fired out, "Pussy-whipped!"

Trevor shot them a look as he took Mandy's hand. "Can we stay just a little longer?"

"They're being so mean to you."

"They're just being guys."

"You're not like that."

"Sometimes, I guess."

"I just want to go."

He sighed, letting go of her hand to scratch his head. "I don't get it. I thought you'd have fun."

"This isn't fun."

"Well, Jesus, Mandy. This is the kind of thing I like to do sometimes. If you don't get that—"

Mandy's eyes stung with his impending ultimatum. If she didn't like him joking around with these jerks, what? She would have to learn to live with it, like their miserable, dispirited girlfriends? Or he would dump her?

Sniffling, she decided she wasn't going to be threatened by some clueless drunk jock — even if she was in love with him. She turned away and stormed off. He stayed by the fire, calling after her. At first, he called her name and then the others started repeating it in mocking, wimpy voices. Their teasing ignited the dregs of toxic masculinity within Trevor.

"Mandy!" When she dared to turn around, willing to return to him, the others laughed. "Just go! You're a real fuckin' drag anyway."

With a quivering lip, she ran. She didn't let him see her crying, but by the time she made it to the highway, she was bawling. Mud stained and soaked her dress, and she abandoned her shoes to the muck. Dirty and sweaty and cold, she walked two hours down the lonely road back to her house. She slipped in before dawn, before her father could wake up to ask about her magical evening — and before the ambulance transported Trevor's lifeless body to the Fisher & Sons Funeral Home.

CHAPTER 5

C haz rolled onto his hands and knees. "I think I'm gonna be sick..."

Mandy pointed him out the door and to the bathroom down the hall. He stumbled out. His large body pinballed off each wall and just about knocked over the vase of dried flowers.

Mandy waited until she heard him retching before she gazed down at the dead man. "I'm sorry," she whispered. "There's nothing I can do. Well..." She looked over her shoulder, and as if to answer her unspoken query, Chaz retched again. "Maybe there is, but I don't think it will work again."

She pushed herself away from the table and went to the phone. She had every intention of calling the police while Chaz was indisposed, but when she glanced back at Robbie, she imagined Trevor the morning after prom — laid out on that very table as her father unzipped the body bag. Mandy covered her mouth, sucking air between her fingers. Blood and beer mingled in the air just as it had wafted off Chaz's breath. Trevor was pale, cold, dead. His fingers were frozen in a death grip around the steering wheel he had been pried away from. His face was bloodied and almost unrecognizable — but Mandy would have known him anywhere. Her father quickly sent her away.

She found out days later that after she left the grad party, he had ditched his friends. They told him not to get behind the wheel and in return he told them to fuck off. He had made a mistake. He was going after her. He loved her. He was sorry. He was mad. He had royally messed up the one good thing in his life that wasn't tied to football.

But his reaction time was impaired by the alcohol in his system. He cut in front of a semi, sideswiped another vehicle, spun out, and crashed into a tree. Dead on impact.

She didn't see Trevor again until the day of the service. Her father left to sort out last-minute details under the assurance that she wouldn't go anywhere near Trevor. She promised.

It was one of the few times she had lied to her father.

She crept into the room where her father had finished with Trevor's makeup. He looked as fresh as a daisy. *Daisy* — the first flower he ever gave her. She beat a fist against her thigh for not keeping it, for not drying it out to preserve it in a scrapbook. She was terrible about keeping mementos.

Wracked with sobs, she threw herself on him. She kept waiting for him to twitch or fidget back to life. But he was still. So still.

She climbed onto the table, wedging her body next to his. She draped one leg over him, her skirt riding up. Holding onto him like a life preserver, she closed her eyes shut and thought about the good times — and not the future that was taken away. She chased down those happy moments in her memory, reliving them over and over. She squeezed the joy and excitement and love out of each one.

Their first time in his truck. His body between her legs, her arms wrapped around him. She didn't let go. She was afraid to slip, to lose him, and then she slowly found her rhythm, moving along with him, matching his pace.

As she clung to Trevor in the cold embalming room, she found her rhythm again. Slowly, slight movements at first, she began to chafe against him. She adjusted her leg, pulling up her skirt. A strange, yet not un-welcome warmth, spread throughout her groin. Her rhythm intensified. She rubbed against him, pressing harder.

His head lolled to one side. She climbed on top of him, turning his face back to hers. She buried herself in the crook of his neck. He smelled of chemicals and makeup. Not like himself at all.

She wept, moaning — a tornado of grief, shame, lust, and bottomless despair.

Her muscles contracted, throbbing wetness. Relief spread through her, followed by mortification. *What have I done? Oh, god...* And yet...

That release in her soul was all she thought about when she quietly shut the door on Chaz and hurriedly climbed the table to straddle Robbie. She hiked up her dress and positioned her most sensitive area against his jutting hip bone. She squeezed her eyes shut and thought of Trevor.

Her long, limp hair fell off her shoulders and over his face. She couldn't hear anything over her increasingly loud panting and thundering heart. The act of stimulation consumed her attention. She lost herself. She was with Trevor now. Robbie was only a proxy.

Tears streamed down her face as she imagined their reunion. She was so close. He was almost right there with her. Closer...

As she was on the brink of pleasure (or perhaps madness), Chaz threw open the door. *"What the holy fuck are you doing?"*

Before she could stop, before she could think, before she could fumble for an excuse, Chaz charged at her. *"Get offa him!"* With a meaty elbow, he knocked her to the floor. She landed hard, but unbroken.

"Fucking weirdo." Chaz stomped over to her, his face twisted into a ghoulish mask. "What the fuck? You sick?"

Mandy didn't know what she was, except heartbroken and humiliated. And now hopeless. She had tried to do a good deed, tried to get the strangers out of her home before her father came back. Now she had just made it worse.

What happened with Trevor had been a freak incident.

Mandy wiped her nose, staring at Chaz's foot as it hovered near her ribs. She waited for the kick. Would he break her ribs or stomp her face in? Maybe he would kill her and end this nightmare. Maybe if there really was a god or heaven, Trevor would be waiting for her.

Probably not.

"Just leave," she told him.

He drew his leg back. His ankle stiffened.

Someone groaned.

Mandy stopped breathing as Robbie gasped. She had done it again.

He's alive.

CHAPTER 6

R obbie opened his eyes. He couldn't focus. The edges of everything were fuzzy. The light above was blinding. But he didn't dare close his eyes again. The last time he did, there was nothing on the other side. Nothing but never-ending darkness.

His stomach lurched. His heart beat sluggishly. He flexed and curled his fingers and toes, rotated his ankles. He was all in one piece, though some of those pieces were worse for wear.

The last thing he remembered was the engine of his BMW revving as he took the corner too fast. And then he blinked. It all happened so quickly. One second he was right-side up and the next he was crumpled up on the ceiling of the car, his neck bent at a funny angle. And then relief. It was over.

Except it really wasn't.

He shifted, groaning. His ribs crackled. His neck felt out of joint. Wherever he was reeked of a stuffy floral scent that made his nose itch. And then Chaz was there, red-faced and blubbering. Fucking Chaz who promised he would be okay to drive and then started playing beer pong with a couple of chicks. So Robbie had to sober up and get behind the wheel.

Robbie blinked. The light was too bright. He turned to look away and a sharp stab fired in his neck down to his gut. He chomped down on his cheek, drawing blood. The coppery taste tainted his mouth as he tried to ask Chaz, "What the fuck happened to my car?"

His BMW M4 was a supermodel compared to all the average and ugly hunks-of-junk on the road. Though it shined next to Chaz's late 2000s Pontiac GTO, the M4 paled in comparison to the M8 he had wanted. His dad promised something better if he finished his degree, but his old man was always making promises he had no intention of keeping.

It was also very likely he didn't expect Robbie to graduate.

If the M4 was truly wrecked, he would have no choice but to replace it with the better model. His dad would have to bend to that logic.

Chaz squeezed him, chanting *ohmygod, ohmygod, ohmygod.* Then he looked back at another person, someone crouched on the ground like an unwanted creature, and said, "He's alive. Holy shit, he's alive."

The light hurt. Robbie dug his palms against his eyeballs. The pressure dulled the intensity but didn't relieve the ache.

He groaned again, struggling to sit up. "Can we go now?"

"Sure, buddy, sure," said Chaz, putting an arm around him. Robbie's legs were unsteady. He didn't want anybody's help, but if he was going to get out, he needed to rely on Chaz. "What do you remember?"

Robbie remembered everything. He remembered that they drove out of the city. They — he — had to get away for the weekend. They got stuck behind a truck with an I HEART ALBERTA BEEF sticker on the rusted bumper. Ramshackle barns dotted the landscape. He hated everything about the rural area surrounding his city, even though his dad lived on a private acreage just beyond city limits. But he never would have ventured out if it hadn't been for Marisol Chu.

She had started pointing fingers. She had changed her mind. Bitches always did. They played cute and frisky until the morning after when the harsh light of day made them rethink the dirty things they had done. The walk of shame really warped a girl's perception of the night before.

Marisol had been all over him until he took her upstairs at the frat house. Then the second he got in her pants, she started pushing him back. But she was laughing the whole time and telling him he was too much. He laughed back, right in her sweaty, paint-ed-up face. She looked like a melting clown. That was hilarious. It was going to be funny, he thought, fucking a clown. *Would she squeak?* he wondered. *Would she honk?* He laughed even harder.

When the stupid little clown tried to scramble away like it was a game, he held her down. No squeaks, no honks. Just pathetic weeping. But girls always cried, which grossed him out. He didn't need her falling in love with him. Christ, he didn't need the emotional baggage.

She left uneventfully and he went to sleep. But something between them hung in the air the rest of the week. She texted him, wanting to talk about "the other night." Robbie ghosted her, trying to ignore her messages and the mutual friends who wanted to talk to him on her behalf.

"You should talk to Marisol. It's important."

"You need to apologize."

"You need to take responsibility."

If it was so important, she knew where to find him. And then the rumors began. People were whispering that he was a creep, a rapist, a monster. He wasn't any of those things. They had it all wrong. He was just an unfortunate young man with a bright future who didn't want to be pressured into a relationship by some psychotic, lovedrunk girl.

Those who were brave enough to approach him demanded he do right by Marisol and leave, and not just for the day. They *actually* expected him to drop out of school entirely. They were out of their minds if they thought *that* was ever going to happen. Robbie had a degree to finish if he was ever going to get his M8.

With their accusations mounting, Robbie decided enough was enough. He texted his buddies for a guy's night out. Only Chaz took him up on the offer.

They loaded up his BMW with cases of beer and ditched the city. Robbie wanted to speed. He wanted to crush beer cans and throw them at road signs. He wanted to feel the wind through his hair and look death in the eye.

He didn't intend to French kiss death by rolling his car.

As Chaz helped him shuffled out of the unfamiliar room, Robbie rubbed his aching neck. He passed a girl, cowering on the floor in her nightdress and robe. She was ghostly pale with dark circles under her wide, watery eyes. Her long, fair hair hung down around her face in a frizzy, unkempt mess.

They made eye contact. Though she looked ill, he couldn't look away.

Weirdo, he thought as Chaz pestered him with questions.

"What?" he growled.

Chaz jostled him as they left the darkened, creaky house. The black sky, covered in sluggish, grey clouds, pressed down on Robbie, reminding him of... *Of what?*

His death.

Chaz broke the oppressive silence. "I thought you were..." He couldn't say it. It was impossible to someone as small-minded as Chaz. "You okay, man?"

Robbie drew a deep, sharp breath. It reminded him that he was still alive. He had been granted a second chance. He had cheated death.

He grinned at Chaz as they drifted away from the house, back to the scene of the accident. Away from the strange house in the middle of nowhere.

"Never been better."

CHAPTER 7

TWO WEEKS LATER...

H e may have cheated death, but Robbie wasn't feeling too well. He could barely roll out of bed and hadn't left his dorm room in days. When he managed to get up, his bones and muscles were too weak to keep him standing. He flopped down at his desk, rallying himself to open his laptop. Once he got that far, he emailed his excuses to his professors.

Finally, one morning, the storm passed and he felt well enough to drag himself to his computer without too much strain. His neck didn't hurt anymore and he could walk on his own two feet again. He saw an email from his dean.

Several emails from his dean.

"Mr. Pendleton, it is imperative that you make an appointment with my office. We have an urgent matter to discuss..."

He scanned the message. UNBECOMING BEHAVIOR. ACCUSATION. UNACCEPTABLE. THIS IS A SERIOUS MATTER. WITHDRAWAL PENDING. Had this email arrived before his accident, Robbie would have gone into panic mode and called his dad to rescue him. His dad knew how to make problems disappear.

On this day, the dean's email only annoyed Robbie, though it was riddled with enough damning phrases that Robbie had no choice but to confront the dean. He got dressed, grabbed his phone, and went downstairs. He passed a few of his dorm neighbors. They gave him dirty looks or avoided eye contact. Marisol's lies had poisoned even more minds.

When he arrived at the faculty offices on campus, he asked to speak to Dean Kirshner.

"I'm sorry," said the pinchy-faced, middle-aged broad behind the front desk. Robbie peered down at her. Her hand flew to her phone, blatantly in the middle of a round of Candy Crush. Her computer screen showed a webpage for discount shoes. She was clearly keeping her seat warm until retirement. "Dean Kirshner is very busy today. I'm afraid you'll have to make an appointment."

Robbie leaned in closely, catching a whiff of her perfume or old lady hand cream. The floral scent took him back to a recent memory of another place and time. *Where was that again?* And a girl. *Who?*

He let the thought slip away, because this broad wasn't afraid, and he *wanted* to make her afraid. He wanted to see her scream.

"Dean Kirshner asked to see *me*," Robbie said. "Robert Pendleton. He said it was urgent."

Giving him a side-eyed look, she typed something into her computer. The screen flickered. A message popped up. She read it silently. Robbie stepped back and crossed his arms, anything to keep his hands from grabbing her I HATE MONDAYS mug and bashing open her skull with it.

He swallowed back the rage that was building. He had never felt so angry about anything before — not since the accident.

The woman looked up. Her face was even more sour than before. "You'd better go right in, Mr. Pendleton."

Robbie wanted to laugh — *Mr. Pendleton is* my dad's *name* — but he brushed her off and walked into the dean's office.

"Have a seat."

Dean Richard Kirshner sat behind his desk with his long, knobby fingers neatly folded on his desk. He was the very picture of administrative excellence: starched shirt, tweed jacket with leather patches on the elbows, and a decorative pipe. It stuck out of his mouth, unlit but satisfying his oral fixation.

Robbie fixated on snatching it from him and stabbing him in the eyeball.

Dean Kirshner cleared his throat and sorted through the paperwork spread across his desk. "A very serious matter has come to my attention..."

Robbie zoned out. He lost track of time. He stared at the professor's salt and pepper beard and imagined punching him in the throat. His fist clenched. *What would it feel like? Would it be enough to make the old buzzard suffocate on his trachea?* Robbie wasn't sure — he wasn't taking any anatomy classes that semester.

Finally, Dean Kirshner asked, "What do *you* think?"

Blinking, Robbie broke away from the strangely pleasant daydream. "Huh?"

"What do you think about withdrawing for the rest of this semester until a proper investigation can be completed?"

He jumped up. "But I didn't do anything wrong! Why do I have to withdraw?"

"Because—" the dean tried to explain.

"No," Robbie snapped. "This isn't happening. M-my dad is gonna kill me!"

"Mr. Pendleton, calm yourself or I will call security to escort you off the premises." The dean casually placed a hand over the phone. He held it there until Robbie settled back down in his chair. "Thank you. Now, let's discuss next steps…"

Robbie already knew what *his* next steps were. So he nodded, pretending to listen, and waited to be dismissed.

As the dean droned on, Robbie zoned out again. Blood rushed to his ears, leaving the rest of his body feeling weak again. His head weighed heavily on his neck, but he grinned when the old buzzard reached across the desk and shook his hand. Startled by how icy it was, the dean advised Robbie to get a coffee on his way home.

"We'll sort out the paperwork soon," he added. "Your probation begins now and continues indefinitely, and I strongly advise that you leave campus so you can avoid any accidental or unnecessary encounters with the … other party. Understood?"

Robbie nodded. *Got it.*

Necessary encounters only.

Dean Kirshner walked Robbie out the door and through the office. Too bad — Robbie wanted to see the old broad one more time. Her head was down and her eyes focused on another round of Candy Crush. He wanted to crush her nose between his teeth like a piece of candy. Snap it off and chew it up.

The door closed on him. He didn't look back. Driven by a gnawing urge, he marched across campus. He had a destination to reach and nothing was going to stop him.

Along the way, he bumped into one of Chaz's buddies. "Hey, man, watch where you're going!"

Robbie ignored him. He kept his head down. The closer he got to the little yellow house on sorority row, the stealthier he had to be. The other housemates would try to protect her, so he had to avoid detection. No witnesses.

It was the middle of the day. Only a few cars were parked on the street — one of them was Marisol's Volkswagen. It looked like a clown car, perfect for the dumb little clown. Robbie bit down on his lip to hold back a laugh. He would save it for Marisol.

He went up the front steps. The old wooden planks creaked under his weight. He tapped on the glass window. *Rat-a-tat-tat.* The house was quiet. He listened, he waited. He turned to look back at the empty street.

The door opened with a sudden rush of energy. Marisol was smiling, ready to greet her guest. But as Robbie revealed himself, she gasped. Before she could close the door in his face, he pushed his arm through and grabbed her by the throat. Forcing her inside, he slammed the door, muffling her shriek.

CHAPTER 8

C haz arrived at the house within minutes of Robbie's panicked phone call — no questions asked.
He raced out of class without a second thought,
though Robbie could have convinced him just as easi-
ly to skip his economics lecture to hang out on sorority row.

He arrived in his conspicuous bright red Pontiac
GTO, parking it in the alley as Robbie had advised.
Again, no questions asked. Chaz did as he was told.

Robbie peered through the lacy front curtains,
watching for any signs that Marisol's housemates were
home early. There was usually a lot more traffic at
this time of day, but Robbie had gotten lucky. No one
showed up. Not yet at least.

Chaz plodded up the back steps to the porch and
knocked on the screen door. Robbie paused before
answering him, listening for any signs of life from the
front. Still no one.

It was showtime.

Covering his face, he let Chaz in. "Oh, god. Oh, god.
Oh, god, man."

Chaz laid a heavy paw on his shoulder, shaking him gently. "What happened, man? What're you even doing here?"

He lowered his hands, hoping he was able to convey enough anguish to be convincing, but not so much that he appeared to be overacting. It was a delicate balance. "Oh, god. I don't know what happened. I just came over here to talk things out with her..."

He led Chaz through the kitchen, down the narrow hall, and up the stairs. Chaz clomp-clomp-clomped, slowing as he rounded the first landing. He gripped the bannister. At the first smear of blood, he let go.

"Oh, shit..."

"I don't know what happened," Robbie lied. "We were talking civilly. We were working things out. And then she invited me upstairs."

He stood at the entrance to Marisol's room. Chaz didn't dare to come any closer. Robbie needed him to see. He needed his help to move the body that he had already wrapped in bloodied sheets. She was ready to go, but Robbie could not haul her downstairs by himself.

Deep down inside, he *wanted* someone to see what he had done, and Chaz was perfect because he wouldn't tell a soul.

With a sob, he leaned against the wall and slid down to the floor. "She said she was going to make me pay. She said she owned me now. I tried to push her off. I tried to make her stop. I did everything I could and then—" He covered his face again. This time he didn't make a sound. He let the ominous silence catapult Chaz to action.

Chaz stepped gingerly over the blood to peer into the room. His eyes watered and he covered his mouth. Robbie bit his knuckle to keep from smirking.

"It was an accident," he whispered, as Chaz backed against the railing.

Trembling, Chaz nodded. "Yeah. An accident."

"I wouldn't hurt her, you know that. It was just a misunderstanding before."

"Totally..."

"I'm not a bad person." Robbie's voice broke, surprising himself.

"I know that, man."

Robbie gazed up at him with dewy, hopeful eyes. "You'll help me, right?"

Chaz said nothing, looking down at his pitiful friend.

"We have to get her out of here. We have to get her some help."

"I-I-I don't know, man."

"You're my best friend," Robbie said. "You saved my life before. Maybe we can save hers too. But we have to hurry."

Chaz bent over, hands on his knees as he gasped for breath. He was either trying to hold back vomit or was about to have a panic attack. Robbie didn't have time for either. He ordered Chaz to grab one end of Marisol's wrapped-up body while he took the other end. They half-carried, half-dragged the dead girl downstairs, through the kitchen, and out the back door. They crammed her in the Pontiac's trunk.

Robbie told Chaz to stay with her while he did a spot check upstairs. He quickly tidied up any drops of blood they had left behind and wiped down the smear in the hallway. He didn't bother wiping down for any fingerprints — he had forgotten what he might have touched, and besides, the sorority house had many guests; it would be difficult to find Robbie's among so many.

When he had done a fine enough cleanup, he collected all the rags and paper towels in a garbage bag and took them out to the car. Chaz sat in the driver's seat, knuckles white on the wheel.

"Let's go," said Robbie.

"Where?" Chaz asked, firing up the engine. It was easier for someone like Chaz to follow directions than to take a step back and think things through.

"I think there's someone who can help us," Robbie said. "But I don't know the way. Do you?"

Robbie couldn't remember the house or much about the strange girl who lived in it, or how they got there, but he remembered something happened to him there. In between periods of sleep, he thought about it. *Obsessed* about it. *I was dead.* He couldn't tell anyone because no one would believe him.

I was dead and now I'm not.

And the strange girl at the house had something to do with it.

Although he didn't need Marisol to initiate that conversation with Chaz, Robbie still had a vendetta against that tattletale bitch, and if the strange girl was actually able to make people come back to life, it wouldn't hurt to bring a test subject.

As the Pontiac fled the city, Robbie rolled down his window and breathed in the late afternoon air. Mingled with the scent of blood, he smelled freedom and possibilities. And an opportunity to not just cheat death but to control it.

"This girl... Do you remember her name?"

"Never got it."

Robbie grinned. He was going to get her name and everything else she had to offer.

CHAPTER 9

M andy was almost home when she spotted a red car parked at her house. It sat crookedly on the path that led to the front door, partially blocking the porch. The engine was running. Exhaust floated out of the tailpipe. By the time she saw the car, it was too late — the driver would have already seen her truck.

She slowed down, keeping her foot over the brake. She peered through the chipped and cracked windshield, watching to see who was waiting for her. Her father was meeting with vendors in the city and wouldn't be back until late. He had not mentioned anything about having any visitors.

Her hands tightened on the wheel. Her molars gnashed together in a futile attempt at a friendly smile. Mandy preferred not to meet with the public, if she could help it. Her father agreed. After what happened with Trevor, it was best if she worked behind the scenes.

The doors of the car swung open. The driver was Chaz. The passenger was Robbie. Mandy's heart seized up. It had been two weeks since they had disrupted her life, and thankfully her father was never the wiser about their presence.

But they weren't supposed to come back — though she had a terrible feeling why they might return.

Something bad had happened.

Weren't they aware of the phrase "buyer beware"? Mandy couldn't control what happened to the person she resurrected. That was the trade-off for having such a "gift." These two fools had to figure it out for themselves. She couldn't get involved in their problems. They had to go away. They had to leave her alone and never come back. If her father found out, she would be taken back to the rest home — or worse — and never be allowed to leave.

The young men came toward her. Chaz put his hands up, indicating that she should stop the truck. Her foot hovered over the gas pedal. If she plowed into them, it would be over. She wouldn't have to deal with them anymore.

But the town would talk. They would definitely lock her up and throw away the key. She couldn't have that. It would break her father's heart.

Robbie stepped in front of the truck. He placed his hands on the hood before she shifted into park. It was like he dared her to try something. Even as Chaz came up to her window and knocked on the glass, she couldn't turn away from Robbie.

He smiled without a hint of light in his eyes.

He was nothing like Trevor. She felt foolish for ever thinking he was.

"We wanna talk to you," said Chaz, looking pale.

Mandy cracked her window the slightest bit. "H-hello."

"We need your help," he said. "Come on out."

He pulled the handle. She had forgotten to lock the door, so it sprang open, protesting with a rusty squeal.

"Umm," she gulped. He reached in and took her by the elbow. His other hand unclipped her seatbelt. "Hey—"

He pulled her out, gently but with enough force to tell her who had the upper hand. She crossed her arms to slough him off. She didn't want to be touched.

"So here's the thing," Chaz said with Robbie standing nearby. "Something happened and we need you to work your ... magic, or whatever, to do it again."

"Do what again?" she mumbled, scowling at the ground.

Chaz huffed. "Do *it.*"

"What?"

He didn't want to say it because it sounded crazy. It *was* crazy, and impossible, and ungodly. But if he didn't say it, it wasn't real, and what he wanted wouldn't come true.

Mandy's gaze shifted upward to look at him. "What happened?"

"Something," he said. "It's not important. We just need you to do it again."

She turned away, hugging herself. "I don't know what you're talking about."

Chaz's big arm came down in front of her, preventing her from walking away and seeking shelter in the house. "Yeah, you do. There was an accident and—"

"Another one?"

He looked at his friend. "She's asking too many questions."

"That's okay," said Robbie. "I've got a few of my own."

Chaz backed off to give them space. Running his hands through his hair, he wandered back toward the car, and then as if repelled by a magnet, he stayed away from it.

Robbie closed the gap between him and Mandy, taking her hand in his. She shrunk away, recoiling not just at the iciness of his touch but the tender way he held her. It was too intimate.

He leaned in, whispering while Chaz was out of earshot. "I know what you did, and now I want to know how."

"I don't know," she whispered back.

"Yes, you do. And you're going to tell—" He cut himself off with a tight smile. "No, you're going to *show* me."

He squeezed her hand, tugging her toward the car. She pulled back. She wasn't going anywhere with him. She wasn't getting in their car. No way in hell. But he was stronger and he wasn't letting go. His grip rubbed her skin raw. Chaz came up behind her. She dug in her heels.

But they didn't open the door and shove her inside. They led her around to the trunk.

Robbie snapped his fingers at Chaz. "Open it."

Chaz hesitated.

"Do it."

Sighing, Chaz reached into his pocket. The keys jangled out. He pressed a button on the remote starter.

A lock unlatched and the trunk popped up. Mandy smelled death before she spotted the body inside.

That was enough for her. She stamped her heel down on Robbie's foot, bashing his toes. She elbowed him, pushed him away, and made a run for it back to the truck.

She jumped inside and slammed the door, expecting an angry face to appear next to her. But Robbie and Chaz remained by the car — by the dead body, blood soaking through the sheet it was wrapped in. Mandy gunned the engine and blasted toward them. But at the last second, her conscience took the wheel and she veered around them.

She steered wildly, spinning around until she was back on the narrow dirt road. A little farther and she was on the highway.

Halfway to town where she could calm down and decide whether or not to call the police and her father, lights flashed behind her. The red Pontiac was coming up fast. It rode her backend. The driver laid on the horn. The sickly colored dashboard lights gave a ghoulish glow to Robbie's face. In the passenger seat, Chaz held on for dear life.

Mandy pressed the pedal to the metal. The truck rumbled, resisting the urgency, then bolted forward. No — it was struck from behind. Mandy looked back again as the Pontiac backed off, but only for a moment. It revved up and hit her.

She was thrust against the steering wheel. She didn't have a second, or a free hand, to put on her seatbelt. It was too late. Trevor hadn't been wearing a seatbelt either. She didn't want to die like that. All she had to do was make it into town and Robbie and Chaz would have to back off. They wouldn't be so brazen as to rear-end her in front of witnesses.

Would they?

Mandy grit her teeth and kept driving. The old truck didn't have the horsepower that their car did. Robbie sped up with a vehicular roar and coasted alongside her. From the passenger side, Chaz waved at her to pull over. His eyes were wide, his face red and sweaty.

Robbie slid his hands over the steering wheel and with a jerk, he rammed against the truck. Fiberglass on metal screeched. Both vehicles swerved, but Robbie had better traction. He forced her onto the shoulder. The more room she gave, the more he took.

The truck's tires left the road, dipping into the ditch. Mandy lost control on the slick grass. *Bang, bang, bang!* She bounced up, hitting her head on the roof. Her tailbone slammed back down on the stiff seat. She grabbed her head, letting go of the wheel. The truck bounced again, spinning out. She struggled to regain control. It was too much, and too late. She pumped the brakes and the truck shuddered to a stop.

CHAPTER 10

They came for her quickly. She was reeling from the accident when Chaz raced up to the side of the truck. He threw the door open, and as he pulled her out, Mandy watched Robbie saunter down the incline to join them. The clouds on the horizon behind him drifted on as if a roadside murder were not about to happen.

Except they didn't kill her. They ordered her to sit down, then mumbled to each other. She strained to hear what they had to say, what they were planning to do with her.

She still had a chance — they were only several yards away from the rickety fence, rusted silo, and a dilapidated barn that belonged to Mr. Pomerleau. That meant they were on his land. He may have neglected the barn all these years, but he was always on high alert for trespassers. All Mandy had to do was play the part of the helpless rag doll and wait.

Robbie pointed at her and snapped at Chaz to, "Just do it already." Whatever *it* was.

She didn't fight when Chaz scooped her up and carried her to the barn. Robbie pried open one of the doors. Everything creaked. Late afternoon light peeked through the rotting boards. Dust sprinkled down, disturbed by their presence.

Chaz grumbled as he pushed past Robbie to find somewhere to set Mandy down. Surrounded by abandoned machinery reeking of oil and rust, he settled for a tractor tire. The ground was cold under Mandy's skirt. She curled her legs up and hugged herself.

Robbie shut the door, trapping them inside.

"So now what?" Chaz asked. "We fucked up her truck in *my* car. I'm gonna lose my license!"

Robbie held up a hand, shushing him. He left Chaz to crouch down in front of Mandy. He balanced himself on the balls of his feet, not wanting to soil the knees of his pants.

"Hi," he said, sticking his hand in her face. "We haven't been properly introduced. I'm Robbie. What's your name?"

Lips pinched together, she decided she wasn't going to tell him anything.

He dropped his hand, letting it dangle between his legs. "That's okay. You don't have to tell me." He reached down into the straw and dirt, brushing away at a piece of corroded metal lost to time. Like a wizened archaeologist making a discovery, he wiped at the wrench gently, thoughtfully. He studied it. "You really don't... Because I can beat it out of you."

Her breath caught. Remembering the dead girl in their trunk, Mandy lost the luxury of acting defiant. Like when they first darkened her door, it was best to give them what they wanted and pray they would go away.

"So," he began again. "What's your name?"

"Mandy," she coughed out.

"That wasn't so bad." He picked up the wrench. "Now, how did you do it?"

"Do what?" she asked carefully.

Casting a glance at Chaz, Robbie leaned in until his teeth grazed her cheekbone. She flinched. He whispered in her ear, "How did you bring me back from the dead?"

Mandy shivered. She didn't know how he could know that — how he could have retained such clarity — but then she didn't have much experience with resurrection. It had been an accidental discovery with Trevor.

His eyes opened following her climax. He groaned. She scrambled to get away, falling to the floor. Tears streaming, she watched in awe as he pushed himself up. He looked around, he sniffed the air, he blinked.

He was alive. It had all been a bad dream. A trick of her mind. She had never lost Trevor. He had always been hers.

On shaky legs, she went to him. She held out a hand. It too shook. She was overwhelmed, flooded with feelings. She grasped his knee. He snarled and—

Robbie throttled her back to the present, his sneering face close to hers.

"If you don't tell me what I want to know, I'm going to fucking kill you."

CHAPTER 11

W hat was there to tell? Girl meets boy. Boy is way out of girl's league but interested. Girl falls for boy. Boy dies in tragic car wreck. Girl has sex with dead boy and brings him back to life. A tale as old as time. But she couldn't tell Robbie that. She hadn't told anyone, not a soul. She had intended to take this secret to her grave. Even when her father had her committed for two years, she stayed mum. The skilled and professional psychiatrists and nurses at the mental health facility couldn't drag the truth out of her — that she brought her dead boyfriend back to life, and that the reason she had been committed was not because she brought him back, but because of what happened next.

Trevor snarled at her before leaping off the table and came after her. He wasn't himself. He almost wasn't human. He clawed at his forearms and stomach and chest and throat and head. He howled in pain. Only when Mandy had time at the "rest home," as her father preferred to call the facility, did she reflect on what Trevor was going through.

He had been embalmed, and the chemicals raged through his insides — poisoning his second chance.

Mandy cried as she ran from him. He snatched a handful of her hair, yanking her off her feet before she could run upstairs. Then he kneed her in the back. She dropped down. He let her go to scratch at his own flesh.

He blocked the stairs, but Mandy got to her feet and raced for the back door. As her hands twisted the knob, Trevor was on her again. His strong arms wrapped around her waist, carrying her into the darkest depths of the house. She grabbed onto the doorframe, kicking him off until she could fling herself into the kitchen. She smacked into the refrigerator, ricocheting off its surface toward the knife rack. She drew the first blade she touched and spun around.

Trevor hunkered in the doorway. He watched her without the slightest hint of recognition on his face. He stepped forward, raising his bloody arms. A violent shudder wracked his body. He bent over, retching. Blood and bile burst onto the floor. He wailed, scratching his throat. His muscles contracted, reminding Mandy of just how big and strong he was — even in death.

She needed something much bigger than a steak knife.

She threw open the drawer and took out her father's meat cleaver. She didn't have a moment to sharpen it or to try to flee to another room to avoid the inevitable. Trevor was on her again.

She swung the cleaver. The blade glided into his left flank. His jaw dropped, saliva dripping onto her shoulder. He held onto the counter on either side of her. She was trapped. She shrank down, pressed against the drawer until the handle left an indent in the small of her back.

Trevor sucked in a sharp breath. For a moment, he was himself again. The same boy who brought her daisies and chocolate, who took her for long rides in his truck. The one who loved her.

The cleaver loosened, sliding out. She exhaled. "I'm so—" *Sorry sorry sorry*. She planned to say it a million times. She was going to say it even if he hated her from this moment on. And that would be fine with her as long as he lived. As long as she could get him to a hospital and not be the one who killed him.

He shifted. His head tilted down, looming over her. He wrapped his hands around her neck, slowly pulling her up until her feet dangled above the floor, above his feet. Then he began to squeeze. She kicked, but he was a statue and she couldn't spare the oxygen. He studied her face as it changed colors — white to red to purple. Her eyes bulged. She choked on his name. He would not let go.

He wasn't going to let her live.

So she swung the cleaver again. It severed his bicep. His tendons and muscles snapped apart. It was like chopping raw chicken, but not quite — the chicken was still moving, and trying to murder her. She hacked again and again. Grunting, he released her. This time she didn't run. She cornered him by the kitchen window. He held up his other hand, the one still attached to his body. She cut it off. It landed with a meaty thud between his legs. She cut those off too.

She didn't stop until he stopped moving.

Only once she had dismembered his entire body did she take stock of what she had done. Her hands cramped. Her dress was soaked, dripping blood. She couldn't see through her tears.

And then her father came home. He was chatting with two other men, hired to transport the body to the church. They almost strolled past the kitchen where the sight of Mandy stole their breaths and likely haunted them for the rest of their lives. They never came back to the Fisher & Sons Funeral Home after that day, and rumor had it that they left the death business entirely.

Mandy had ruined more than one life that day — her father's included.

But at that moment, she wasn't worried about anyone else. She stayed by Trevor's side until her father planted his hands on her shoulders and led her away.

She tried to explain — that she had to make sure he was dead, that he wasn't going to come back — but her father wouldn't hear it. He knew Trevor's death had broken her heart — but her mind too? He accepted that his business might be ruined after this, but he couldn't lose his only child too.

So he called in several favors from upstanding members in the community and on the town council. They worked something out that would ensure Mandy didn't need to see the inside of a jail cell or have to stand before a judge. Trevor's funeral was delayed for reasons that Mr. Fisher concocted (though in reality, he needed time to undo the damage Mandy had done), even offered his services at no cost to the family and then delivered his daughter to the rest home up north. She didn't fight her fate. It was better than she deserved for what she had done to Trevor.

But *how* did she do it?

She dwelled on that question for the next two years. She wasn't sure *how*, but she kept coming back to that desperate, dirty neediness she had for his body. For *him*. But was it Trevor or was it something within her? She wouldn't know for sure until Robbie and Chaz showed up at her house.

Maybe it was a gift, but it was also a curse. And she should never have used it again.

CHAPTER 12

Robbie shook her until her head bounced off the tractor tire. She was too frightened to scream or beg him to stop. She just wrung her hands in her lap and hoped his meltdown would be over soon.

"TELL ME!" he roared. Spit flecked across her face. She cowered, unable to shrink down any farther or blend into the rubber tire, disappearing forever.

Chaz intervened, pulling Robbie away. "Stop it, man. Jesus Christ. You're scaring her." His wide eyes revealed that he was also scared. "Why are you acting like this?"

Teeth bared, Robbie launched at his friend. Chaz put up his dukes and clocked Robbie on the side of the head. Robbie wobbled, surprised. He spun around. The rusty wrench in his hand had just enough shine to reflect a bit of light at Mandy, who caught the glimmer in his eye. He covered his face, hiding his grin.

Chaz put down his fists. "Oh, shit. Robbie, man. Oh, shit. I'm so sorry, dude. I didn't mean to—"

He may not have meant to hit Robbie, but Robbie meant it when he cracked Chaz's sorry face with the wrench. Chaz made a wet *oof* sound. Robbie went in for more. Another hit. Teeth rattled loose and scattered across the barn. Robbie wailed on Chaz, forcing him to the ground. Chaz squirmed, but he had nowhere to go. Robbie didn't stop until he had beaten his friend to a pulp.

Mandy screamed silently into her palms. But it wasn't the time to be a wallflower. She scrambled to her feet and ran to the opposite end of the barn. She might not be able to outrun Robbie, but if she had the element of surprise, she could get a head start. And maybe, just maybe, Mr. Pomerleau would meet her halfway.

However, Robbie wasn't surprised and he was faster than he looked. He was on her in seconds, weaving his fingers through her hair. He twisted and tightened the strands around his knuckles, jerking her back.

"Where do you think you're going?"

He dragged her back, past the big tire, and shoved her down next to Chaz. She rolled over, ready to spring back up and try again, but the sight of Chaz's meaty, broken skull froze her. She had seen dead bodies before, but not like this. This was...

"It was an accident," Robbie said, standing over her. He gripped the wrench, dripping with blood and gore. "You saw what he did." Each word exited his mouth without any emotion. "He hit me."

"And the girl?" she whispered.

"What girl?"

How does someone forget about a dead girl in their trunk? "The one in your car."

He shrugged. "What about her?"

"Was she an accident too?"

"Chaz is very clumsy," he lied. "Big, dumb jock."

Mandy straightened out her skirt, covering her legs. She wouldn't risk bolting now, not when his eyes were on her. No distractions this time. She was going to have to find another way to escape.

"What do you want?"

"I told you," he replied. "I know I was dead and you brought me back. I want you to tell me what you did."

"I don't know."

He laughed hollowly and smacked the wrench into his opposite palm. "Bullshit."

"It's true. I don't really understand it."

"Then let's figure it out together, shall we?"

"Your friend needs help."

"No, he doesn't. He's fucking dead. He can wait."

She opened her mouth to offer another excuse. He grabbed the back of her collar, choking her ever so slightly. "I *will* kill you," he promised. "So you can either tell me or..." He pushed her against Chaz. Her skirt absorbed his blood, touching her skin. "... Or give me a demonstration."

"No!" she cried.

With a laugh, released her, just enough to give her some breathing room. "So you'll tell me?"

"I don't really understand it, but..."

She told him. She left out the touchy-feely parts, about her love for Trevor and her loyalty to her father. She gave Robbie the barest bones of the story because he was the type who would gnaw on the bones and suck out the marrow. *Give 'em an inch and they'll take a mile*, her father liked to say.

61

After she told him everything she knew, she stared at her shaking hands. She couldn't look at him. She was wanton, sick, depraved. Centuries ago, she would have been burned at the stake.

"Huh." He rubbed his lips. "Well, that's quite a story... Can you prove it?"

Her fingers worried the edge of her skirt. "I don't think I can."

"How do you know if you don't try?" He pointed to Chaz's body.

She shook her head. Aside from requiring the optimal conditions to be aroused enough to act on her urges or that she was being threatened at wrench-point by a wild-eyed lunatic, there was the practical matter of Chaz not having much of a head left. His brain matter oozed all over the ground.

"He's not..." She winced. "He doesn't have a head."

"So? My bones were busted." He raised up his pant leg to show her — nothing. He was fine. Healed. "I got better."

"Yes, but ... with Trevor, he'd been embalmed. He didn't come back as good as you."

He snorted. "First time anyone's called me good."

"It just won't work," she continued. "If there's anything wrong before I try it, they might come back wrong. Or worse."

He pouted. "You said you've only done it twice."

She raised her chin defiantly. They both knew what she was getting at. If Robbie had been a raging psychopath before his death, he was going to be the same raging psychopath after too. Or worse.

He stomped his feet, kicking up straw and dirt. He bashed the wrench against the ground, spiraling into another adult-sized tantrum.

"BRING HIM BACK NOW!"

"I can't!" she screamed.

The barn fell silent. Dust sprinkled down. A breeze made the walls creak. A truck engine rumbled in the distance, getting closer.

Robbie placed the wrench head under Mandy's chin and tipped her head up. Frenzy danced in his eyes. "Bring. Him. Back. *Now.*"

"I can't," she pleaded. "I have to be able to, to..."

"To what?"

"To ... you know ... climax."

He laughed. "Who cares? Just fuck him. Do it now."

"That's not how it works."

He got down on one knee, scraping the wrench down the side of her neck until he knocked her on the collarbone. "I don't care. Just make it happen, or you're gonna look like him in the next five seconds."

Mandy glanced at Chaz. He wasn't in any kind of condition to come back to life. Dismemberment, decapitation — those deaths were final. Any attempt made would only degrade and humiliate her, and then Robbie would kill her anyway. Might as well just skip to the end.

She opened her mouth to tell him *no* when the barn door opened.

Old Mr. Pomerleau had arrived as expected. Under a navy blue puffer vest, he wore a flannel shirt tucked into his saggy jeans. Stepping inside the gloomy barn, he tipped up his trucker hat at the sight of them.

The wet tobacco mess in his gums slipped out at the jaw-dropping sight of Chaz's crushed skull and mutilated face.

"What is going on here?"

CHAPTER 13

"**W**hat are you people doing on my property?" Pomerleau's knees cracked and clicked as he shuffled closer. "What happened to that boy?"

"Go," Mandy whispered. "Please go."

"This is *my* property and I'm not going anywhere 'til one of you hooligans tells me what's going on."

Mandy looked to Robbie for permission before standing up. He clasped his hands behind his back, watching their interaction like a curious puppy and not the savage cur that he truly was.

"Just go, Mr. Pomerleau," she said. "I'll take care of this."

He leaned in, squinting his rheumy eyes. "That you? Fisher's girl?"

"We didn't mean to bother you," she said, hoping his poor eyesight and advanced years combined with the dim light in the barn would be enough to confuse him. If she spoke calmly, perhaps he would begin to question everything and return to his house.

Mandy slipped an arm through his, guiding him back outside. Lingering behind, Robbie watched them go.

Mandy inhaled the fresh air. She wanted to grab the old man and run to his truck. But the old man hobbled along, his knees too weak to hustle.

"Who's with you," he asked. "I don't know him. He one of Jake's boys?"

"No, sir. He's—"

The barn door opened. Mandy froze. They were too far from the idling truck to run for it. Pomerleau turned just as Robbie hit him with the wrench. Blood seeped from his nose. He fell to the ground, moaning. Then Robbie kicked him in the ribs.

"Old son of a bitch," he muttered, raising his foot

"Please, no..." Pomerleau groaned. He let out a strangled cry when Robbie's foot came down.

Mandy ran. It was her only chance. The tall grass scratched up her legs. The field ahead was riddled with prairie dog holes. If she dared to look back, one of the holes would snag her and break her ankle.

Robbie ran after her, panting. He hooked her shoulder and spun her around. She tripped. He bumped into her, then pushed her down.

"Fucking bitch," Robbie spat. He wiped the spittle from his lips. The bloody wrench remained in his hand, like a new appendage.

Mandy laid in the grass, digging her nails into the soil. She tried to catch her breath, she tried to think. Pomerleau had been her last chance. She was either going to be murdered on the edge of the old farmer's property or...

Or something much worse.

"You're in a shitload of trouble," Robbie said. "That old bastard is dead because of you."

"Me? But you—" *Killed him.*

"No one knows me here. Not even you. You'll be the one they're after." *The police. The town. Her father.*

"No..."

"Don't you read the news? The police don't care about solving crimes. They just want to lock someone up and forget about it. All they need to do is arrest you and that'll be enough."

Mandy didn't think that was true, but then she remembered how hard her father fought to keep her out of jail. How he put her away in a special facility so she could "get better," but never once asked her about what had happened. He likely didn't want to know. She didn't blame him. He wouldn't have been able to comprehend what was really wrong with her.

And that was just it. She had a history of violence. She had chopped up the body of Trevor Hardisty, the town's beloved high school football star. Everyone knew it, even if it wasn't on any official records. The town weirdo snapped and butchered one of their beloved sons. It was as if she actually murdered him (which was kind of true — there was always a bit of truth in every legend).

Robbie was right, more than he knew. The police would come for her, and this time, she wouldn't get a free pass. They would lock her away. The town would snicker and say "told ya so" to each other, and her father would be shamed and run out of business.

She stared across the field at the setting sun.

Robbie sat down beside her, draping his arm over her shoulders. His touch gave her the creeps. "I might be able to help. But you're going to have to help me."

CHAPTER 14

Mandy peeled her forehead away from the glass. She opened her eyes. Everything was black except for the dotted highway line disappearing under the Pontiac's front end. She didn't remember dozing off or where they were headed. The last thing she recalled was that Robbie led her back to the red car on the side of the road, near the truck. He ordered her to get in the passenger seat. The inside smelled of death.

Mandy hesitated, unable to forget about the dead body in the trunk. Robbie nudged her. "Go on."

When she settled in, he reached behind her and slammed her head against the dashboard. Stars exploded behind her eyes and then she drowned in them until blackness swallowed her up.

No wonder her head hurt.

She tried to stifle a groan as she touched her face, surveying the damage. Not that she was much of a looker to begin with. Average would have been a glowing compliment. Mandy was plain, like a houseplant that didn't get enough water but still rose up to greet the sun every day.

Yet somehow Trevor thought she was special.

What an idiot, she thought, tears springing to her eyes. Although she wasn't certain if Trevor was the idiot for falling for her and driving drunk, or if she was the idiot — for everything else.

Sniffling, she wiped her nose.

Thrumming his fingers on the steering wheel, Robbie gave her sly glance. "What're you sniveling about? I told you, I can take care of this."

She shrugged, gazing out the window and trying to avoid Robbie's green-tinted reflection in the glass. Trees whipped by and in the distance, the bright lights of the city twinkled. But they weren't going to the city. Mandy regained enough of her bearings to know which road they were on — a secondary highway that would eventually connect to the main route into the city. But if they were traveling north, which was where the city lay, it was a trick. The road looped north before veering east, away from bright lights and urban sprawl, which meant Robbie wasn't taking her where there would be a lot of people. He was isolating her.

"Where are we going?" she squeaked.

He reached over and squeezed her thigh. "Don't worry about it."

She smacked his hand away. "Don't touch me."

"Hey, you started it." He gripped the steering wheel and kept his eyes on the road.

They drove in silence for a while. Mandy pondered how badly it would hurt if she tried rolling out of the vehicle. Would she fall under the back wheel and get her head crushed? Would the road scrape her skin off, leaving her as one big, open wound? Would Robbie come back for her? Maybe, probably, and yes.

As she began to envision another ending to that scenario, Robbie spoke again.

"Why me?" He paused, swallowing. "Why'd you bring me back? I was dead, right?"

"Yes."

"So why then?"

She focused on the highway, the lines racing by. Ahead, a man jogged down the road. The headlights lit up his back. He slowed, stopped, and turned around. He covered his eyes from the brightness, and as the Pontiac sped past, Mandy saw Trevor. She grabbed onto the door handle, craning her neck to see him, to make sure he wasn't an illusion.

She wanted to tell Robbie to pull over. She twisted back around — and up the road a little ways was another man. He too stopped on the side of the road to watch the car go by. He too had Trevor's face. And the next man on the road. And so on. Each one caught in a silent scream as the car passed.

Finally, she let go and slumped down in her seat. The seat belt cut across her throat, but she didn't adjust her posture, afraid she might hallucinate another Trevor.

Robbie snapped his fingers. "Hey! Are you listening? Why me?"

She rubbed her head, wishing this night would end. It had only just begun. "I don't know. I guess ... you reminded me of someone."

"Your boyfriend?"

"I thought you looked like a good person."

Robbie snickered. "Bet you wish you'd kept your damn legs closed, huh?"

"I didn't want you to ruin your life."

"Because life is a precious gift and all that bullshit? What a joke."

"It's not a joke."

"What's a *joke* is you fucking dead guys. How do they even get it up for you? Aren't they all dead and ... you know ... soft...?"

"Yes."

"So how does it work? You just cram their limp dicks inside you?"

She sighed, face burning and headache pounding. This was not a conversation she ever wanted to have. "There are ways to have sex that don't involve penetration, you know."

"None that matter."

"Then you'll never understand," she muttered.

"What'd you say?"

"Nothing."

He shook his head. "Girls like you think you know everything. Think you're better than me. Well, I just think it's funny that now you need *my* help. You have to rely on *me*. So if you want to stay out of jail, you're going to do everything I say."

The car turned sharply onto a hidden road. Thick bushes kept it hidden, though the leaves were drying up, dying, and falling off. The road was littered with death and decay. Mandy looped her fingers around the door handle. Just one tug and she could pop out.

As if reading her mind, Robbie snatched her hand. Their fingers interlocked. The veins in his forearm bulged, strength coursing through his body.

"But don't worry," he said, teeth gritted. "You're mine now. I'll keep you safe. I promise."

The road narrowed to a dirt trail. They followed it to a wrought-iron gate and a guard station. Robbie waved to the uniformed man inside. "Hey, Henry." The security guard gave a nod and hit the button that opened the gates. Smirking, Robbie cruised right past.

Mandy stared in awe — not just at her missed opportunity to cry out for help, but at the sight of the sprawling, perfectly manicured lawn stretching out around a ridiculously opulent fountain and the white mansion beyond it.

She pressed her face to the window. "What is this place?"

He drove up to one of the four garage bays and parked. He shut off the engine, gazing over her shoulder. "Home."

CHAPTER 15

The house looked like it belonged to a sexy billionaire in one of those Harlequin romance books that were always left behind on coffee tables at the rest home. Mandy had tried to read one or two, but she couldn't get past the improbability of a billionaire falling in love with a complete nobody and wanting to give her everything. But for a brief moment, she wondered if that was what was happening here. Was Robbie going to give her everything? Not likely.

Robbie tightened his fist around her hand. She winced, trying to separate from him, but he refused to let go.

"Before you get any ideas," he said, "these are the some ground rules. First off, you're going to keep your mouth shut. No blabbing about everything that's happened. If you do, I know where you live. I'll stake out your house until someone comes home and then I'll slit their fucking throat. You got that?"

She nodded slowly, careful not to make any sudden movements.

"Good. Here's the plan. We're going to meet my dad. I'm going to tell him what you can do and if he thinks you're worth his time, he's going to help you. But if you act like a bitch, you're on your own."

Mandy considered that possibility. She didn't know what Robbie and his dad had in store for her, but she was almost certain turning herself in would be the smart thing to do, even if it hurt her father or meant she had to go to jail. But it was too late to change her mind. Robbie wasn't going to let her go to the police. Not now. He would kill her before that could happen because he was in even more danger than she was.

But she nodded in agreement and let him continue.

"Great," he said. "Be a good girl for me and we'll help you. But if you try running away, my old buddy Henry back there will shoot you dead and then I'll tell the cops that you tried to extort me after killing my pals Chaz and Marisol."

She shivered, thinking of that poor girl locked in the trunk. What had *she* done to deserve Robbie's wrath?

"Any questions?"

"You can't tell your dad," she blurted.

"Can't tell him what?"

"My secret."

"Have to. That's one of the rules."

"But—"

He clenched her hand. "I can't help you on my own. My dad has connections, so we have to work with him."

She wanted to ask if he was like her father, under-standing and kind. Her father had a big heart. He cared about people, dead or alive. He always did his best for them and treated them with respect. But her father wasn't going to be able to get her out of trouble this time.

She needed someone ruthless.

"I don't want people to know about me," she whispered.

He chuckled. "That's too bad. Because either my dad's going to know or the cops will. Your choice."

She didn't have a choice. Option number two also meant Robbie would kill her father.

"Fine," she muttered. "Let's talk to your dad."

He got out of the car. She waited until he came around to open her door, like a weird courtship dance. The driveway was paved with a million little stones and smoothed over until there was not a crack. As she admired the artistry of the ground she now walked on, Robbie jogged up to the garage door and punched in a code. He waved her over as the door rose up.

She glanced back at the car, wondering about the girl — Marisol — still inside.

"Come on," Robbie barked.

Mandy would worry about her later.

Inside was the tidiest and whitest garage she had ever seen. She was so accustomed to visiting her father's friends in their farm workshops with oil and paint splatters on the floor and tools scattered about haphazardly, disassembled vehicles on lifts waiting for parts and attention. Robbie's garage was just for show, a place to park vehicles that cost more than her father's house and business were worth.

The walls were white, the floor was a light cement (practically white), and in the farthest bay was a white

Jaguar. Tools were neatly hung and sorted on a white pegboard. Her eyes landed on a hatchet, sharp and clean. She would never reach it in time.

Robbie grabbed her by the elbow and led her out into the hallway. A cluster of expensive vases sat in a corner for no reason other than for decorative purposes. The scent of oranges and lavender was sprinkled in the air.

When she spoke, her words echoed off the bare walls. "Is this where you live?"

"Rule number one," he growled. *"Keep your mouth shut."*

She pressed her lips together and nodded.

He took her by the hand, hurrying down the hallway. Mandy only caught brief glimpses of each room. One had a pool table and smelled of cigars. The next was empty save for two mats on the floor — a yoga studio? Another was a formal dining room surrounded by dark wood panels on the walls. Finally, they spilled out into an open-concept, sunken living room. But they didn't stop there.

He led her up a set of stairs that split through the kitchen and living room. All the lights were on but nobody appeared to be home. The deeper into the house they went, the louder Mandy's heart pounded in protest. She tried to swallow, but her throat tightened.

On the second floor, she resisted being pulled along. Her pace began to lag. Robbie was too strong and too determined to notice. He pressed onward. Along the way, they passed bedrooms, a bathroom, and a washer-dryer combo inside a closet.

At the end of the hall was a set of double doors. Robbie stopped to stare at them, letting go of Mandy's hand. He hesitated before raising his fist to knock, whispering to her, "Stay behind me and don't say a goddamn thing."

He knocked and a moment later, a gravelly voice welcomed them from the other side.

"Come in."

CHAPTER 16

R obbie twisted the doorknob, pushing his way in. It was the only room not lit up like a stage. A dark, cavernous, almost cozy office. A fireplace crackled with heat and light. A man about Robbie's height leaned an elbow on the mantle and sipped from a whiskey glass.

Across the room, a painfully skinny woman in a grey suit and matching heels sat on a white leather couch, one leg crossed over the other and a tablet balanced on her knee. She didn't look at the door, too focused on taking dictation from the man at the fireplace.

"Dad—" Robbie began.

The man held up a finger and continued speaking to the woman. "Cancel my Monday appointment with Jefferson. I'd like to find another time to give him a kick in the ass."

Robbie's dad had sharp, chiseled features — jaw, chin, shoulders, torso. A hard man within a hard frame. He didn't share Robbie's cherubic face. His brows were black, his hair silver. He slid his glasses off, tracing the arm along his lips, and bit down, revealing a perfect set of teeth.

Mandy felt compelled to expose her neck to this man and urge him to bite her too. She wiped her sweaty palms on her skirt.

Robbie waited until his dad wrapped up his orders to the lovely assistant. Then he dismissed her. She stood up, and with only a passing glance at Robbie, sauntered out of the office.

Instead of embracing his son, Robbie's dad polished off his drink and took a seat behind a large oak desk. He motioned for Robbie and Mandy to take a seat.

"What's this about?" he asked, resting his head against two pointed fingers.

Robbie gulped. "Dad, I want you to meet Mandy."

His dad shifted slightly, reaching across the desk to extend his hand to her. "You must be Mandy. I'm Robert Pendleton II. But please, call me Robert."

Mandy doubted she could do that. Besides, two Robbies? Great. She shook his hand, too jittery to do anything else. Once he was done scrutinizing her grip and handshake, he settled back down on his side of the desk.

"So what's this about?" he asked his son with a heavy sigh. "Are you engaged? Pregnant? What's the deal here?"

"Nothing like that." Robbie swiveled in his seat to gaze at Mandy, making her skin crawl. "Mandy is ... special."

"A lot of girls are special, son," he replied. "And then they become women and ruin your life." He briefly glanced at Mandy. "No offense."

Mandy kept her head down. She couldn't take offense even if she wanted to. She had to sit there and listen as two powerful men talked shit about her and her gender.

"She's not just some random girl," Robbie insisted. "She's got this thing she can do. It's a gift, really. No— Like a *miracle.*"

"I'm sure," said Mr. Pendleton, drolly. "But I'm busy and need to finish up here, so…" He nodded toward the door. He was dismissing them.

Robbie stood up, fighting the urge to leave, to do as his father implied. "No, Dad, wait. Hear me out. This is a *business opportunity.*"

Mr. Pendleton frowned. "I'm not interested in an illegal prostitution ring. Besides, I think you could also do a little better than Mandy here… No offense."

Mandy stayed silent.

"No, it's not that. Mandy can bring people back from the dead."

Stroking his chin, Mr. Pendleton eyed her up. He slowly broke into a grin and chuckled in the same dark way Robbie had before.

"Son," he began. "I heard about what happened at school. I know all about your trouble with that girl— What's her name? Mary something?" He nodded at Mandy. "This isn't her, is it?"

Marisol.

"Girls are always going to make up lies to keep you around. You're a Pendleton, that's just how it goes. But you have to keep your nose clean and your dick in your pants. And you need a better 'crazy bitch detector,' or you're going to be running from this kind of trouble your whole life."

"But—"

Mr. Pendleton snapped his fingers, silencing his son. "No, listen. I can figure a way out of this mess... We'll pay the girl off, transfer her to another school, something like that... But don't come crawling in here with some bullshit story about dead people. I don't want to hear it. It's a fucking waste of my time."

Robbie grasped Mandy's hand, nearly crushing her bones. She grit her teeth, unable to pull away. *You're hurting me!* she wanted to cry — just as Robbie let go.

In a sudden burst, he kicked his dad's desk, rattling everything on top — the computer, the whiskey glass, the neat little cup of pens, the banker's lamp. Mr. Pendleton withdrew, his face an unreadable, cold mask.

Then Robbie picked up the glass and hurled it at his dad's head. He missed by inches.

Mr. Pendleton sucked in a sharp breath. A hand flew over his heart. "Jesus Christ! What the hell are you doing?"

"You never fucking listen to me!" Robbie screamed.

"I listen!" Mr. Pendleton shouted back. "You never say anything worth hearing!"

"Son of bitch!"

Robbie climbed over the desk. His feet smashed the computer to the floor. Mr. Pendleton cried out, more pissed off about his expensive system getting destroyed than his enraged son attacking him. He cold-cocked Robbie, sending him to the floor. Robbie didn't get up. He moaned in a puddle on the other side of the desk.

Mr. Pendleton cradled his own hand. The knuckles were split, swelling up. He collapsed in his chair as dramatically as if he took the punch. "Get this piece of shit out of here," he ordered Mandy, waving them away.

CHAPTER 17

The Pendleton men's problems were too much for Mandy to bear. Why did men's squabbles have to fall on women to repair and tend to? She considered leaving them to hash it out — and marching right out of the house, down the long dirt path, past Henry the security guard, and all the way back home. She could have kissed her father goodnight and passed out in her room.

Well, it was a nice thought anyway.

Instead, she helped Robbie out of his dad's office. With one arm under his shoulders, she carried him to his room using his mumbled directions and eased him down onto his bed. She crossed her arms as Robbie buried his head in his hands.

While Robbie wallowed in self pity, she studied his room. The walls were painted dark forest green and much of the decor matched or complemented the color, like the green and brown plaid bedspread and the paintings of mountains on the walls. There was a sports team pennant pinned above his desk, but otherwise no personal effects. He had no photos of friends or family, no posters hanging on the wall, nothing that showed he cared about anyone or anything, even before his death. A hollow room for a hollow person.

Perhaps it wasn't Mandy who brought him back "wrong"; maybe *he* was the one who had been wrong from the start.

The silver lining of that epiphany was that she hadn't ruined Trevor — it really had been the embalming fluid that drove him mad.

She sighed.

Robbie glared at her through his parted fingers, digging into his forehead. "What the fuck's your problem?"

She unfolded her arms and let them hang by her sides. "Nothing... I think I should go to the police."

In her heart, after meeting his dad, she knew he was never going to do that. He had so much more to lose than her.

"You're not going anywhere."

Her eyes darted to the door.

Robbie stood up, cutting off her last chance to escape. He snapped his fingers in her face until she looked into his bloodshot blue eyes. *"Look at me."* He leaned in close. His sour breath puffed against her face. "He doesn't want you. *I* don't want you. So what good are you now, huh?"

She shook her head, unsure how to answer his question — when he punched her in the gut. His fist plowed all the air out of her. She couldn't even draw a breath to cough. As she doubled over, he drove an elbow down into her shoulder blade.

"Fucking bitch," he spat. "Useless, fucking..."

He shoved her into his open closet. She stumbled against the coat hangers, falling through the limp, unhelpful clothes until she found purchase against the wall. He kicked her. Her legs dropped out from under her body. Sliding down to the floor, she raised her hands up to defend herself. A shoebox dropped down from above and a heavy pair of men's shoes clonked the top of her head. She cried out. He slapped her across the face.

She flinched.

Reaching down, he pinched her face until her jaw threatened to crack. "I'm so tired," he whispered, "of bitches like you thinking you know everything. You don't know *shit*... Say it."

"What?"

"Say you don't know shit," he hissed.

"I don't know shit." Her voice warbled nervously.

He shoved her and her head struck the wall. "Fucking right."

She rubbed her jaw. There had to be a way out of the house. Perhaps the window over his bed. If she could get up there and flip the lock, she might be able to climb out — except they were on the second floor and it would be one hell of a drop.

She considered screaming her lungs out. Either Mr. Pendleton or his assistant would have to come running, or what about the security guard? Wasn't it his job to help people? But he likely wouldn't make it in time before Robbie killed her and found a way to cover it up.

She was trapped. All she could do was wait and see. She swallowed and looked down at her feet.

"Hey." He snapped his fingers in her face. "Chill. This isn't over. I'll talk to my dad in the morning." Standing up, he let out a big yawn. "Tomorrow, first thing. If my dad for sure won't help, then ... you're gonna have to do it."

"Do what?"

He gazed in her direction with heavy-lidded eyes. Not quite looking at her, as if she wasn't human. As if she didn't matter. "What I tell you."

He shut the closet doors on her. On the other side, he jerry-rigged a "lock" using the rope from a bathrobe. He tied it tightly, then tested it, leaving a gap that he could hardly squeeze his hand through. With a satisfied grunt, he stepped back and admired his handy work.

"Tomorrow," he told her, with another yawn. "If this doesn't work out, you're gonna have to bring them back. All of them."

CHAPTER 18

While Robbie slept peacefully in his bed, Mandy spent the next hour shivering in the dark. Her teeth chattered together and her hands trembled. She fiddled with her skirt and wrung her hands together, but neither calmed her down.

If she didn't do what he wanted, Robbie was either going to kill her or starve her to death in his closet.

A woman's scream pierced through the silent house, disrupting Mandy's mounting panic with a new fear. Mandy covered her ears, bracing for her predicament to worsen.

Groaning, Robbie rolled over and scratched his scalp. Through the parted closet doors, he cast an icy look in Mandy's direction. When the scream echoed out again, from beyond the room, down the long hallway, it was clear Mandy wasn't the perpetrator. Still, he scowled as if she were at fault.

He climbed out of bed and shuffled to the door, leaving his captive alone in the dark. He poked his head outside. High heels clicked on the floor, coming closer, getting louder. Mandy pressed against the wall, momentarily relieved to be in a place of hiding, but all the more terrified to be discovered in a vulnerable position.

She had to get out of the house before it was too late.

"Oh my god! Oh my god!" Mandy couldn't see, but suspected the woman's breathy voice belonged to Mr. Pendleton's glamorous assistant. "Oh my god, oh my god," she chanted, as if conducting an incantation.

"What?" Robbie asked, stepping into the hall. He closed the door behind him. "What's all the screaming about?"

"Oh my god, your father!"

"What about him?" Robbie's voice became smaller and farther away, as the two rushed down the hall.

The house grew quiet again. Mandy waited, listened. A door opened and shut. The woman started to weep. Another door slammed. Robbie spoke again.

"Don't call 911."

"What?"

"Just wait."

"W-why?"

"*I'm* gonna do it myself. Just lemme get my phone."

The door to his bedroom flew open and Robbie breezed in. He shut the door and leaned against it.

Mandy waited on tenterhooks.

"He's dead," Robbie croaked.

"Who?" she squeaked, even as she recognized the stupidity of her question.

"My dad. He just ... just dropped dead or something."

An icy sensation trickled down deep in her gut.

"I just have to find the..." he muttered on his way out again.

That was enough for Mandy. Well aware of what he would soon ask of her, she pushed on the closet, parting the doors enough for her small hand to reach through the gap. Her fingers fussed with the tie, loosening the knot a bit — when Robbie barged back in. She had only freed one loop.

She retracted her hand and sat on it, praying he hadn't seen her.

He was breathing hard now, pacing back and forth. He toyed with his phone, typing and deleting numbers — *9-1-1* — all the while whispering to himself. He had plans and ideas, something about money, freedom. Mandy couldn't follow.

Nerves shot, she burst out, "I won't do it!"

He stopped and turned to the closet.

"You won't do what?"

She bit her tongue.

He cocked his head to one side, cracking something in his neck. "Are you afraid I'm going to ask you to help my dad?" His eyes widened gleefully, spying on her through the gap. "You think I'm going to beg you to bring him back? To work your little magic?"

"He'll come back wrong," she promised.

He crouched down in front of her. "Wrong... You think *I* came back wrong. You think I'm fucked up." He punched the doors, striking at her like a cobra. *"What's wrong with me, Mandy? What's wrong with me? Huh? Tell me. What did you do?"*

"Please stop," she begged. "Please..."

She wanted to curl up on her side and die.

Getting to his feet, he shook the doors. The banging startled Mandy back to reality.

"Nothing's wrong with *me*, Mandy," he said. "You're the one who's fucked up. You fuck dead guys. You're one sick bitch. I'd love to watch them take you away in handcuffs, watch you rot in prison. *You're* the one who's fucked up — not me."

"But your dad..." Her love for her own father made her heart feel heavy. He would be worried sick that she wasn't at home. Would he call the police? Would he go searching for her in the dead of night? Would her absence break his heart? "If he was my father—"

"Fuck your father," he spat. "I don't care." Robbie pointed at the door with his good arm. Down the hall and back to the office, where Mandy imagined Mr. Pendleton laid on the floor, waiting for help. Even in death, he needed someone to care for him. "My old man was a real son of a bitch — but a son of bitch worth three hundred million dollars. Stocks and bonds and all that shit — it's *mine* now."

He turned his attention back to his phone. He started to dial 911 again, but deleted the digits. "Better wait," he muttered, glancing her way. "If they get here too soon, they might actually help him."

And Mandy too. She was going to scream to high heaven when the EMTs arrived. She cleared her throat to test her voice. She had never been loud in her life, not even on the playground as a child or when she saw Trevor's body on the slab. She had never actually used her voice to speak up before.

Robbie stuffed the phone in his pocket. He marched to the door and— Mandy held her breath. Robbie returned to the closet and tested the tie. He hadn't noticed that Mandy had loosened one of the knots.

As he peered inside at her, his eyes had a faraway look. "I have a question."

"S-sure?"

"Did you love your father?"

"I do, yes."

"You lived with him?"

"I do..."

"Will he miss you?"

Iciness clutched her heart. His questions... His use of past tense...

Flooded with panicked thoughts, she didn't answer, but that didn't matter to Robbie. He had already made up his mind. "No. I don't need you to help my dad. But before I can call an ambulance, I need you to clean up this mess you've made. You're going to bring the others back. You're going to fix everything."

CHAPTER 19

R obbie untied the knot. His blunt fingers worked on the fabric until it was loose enough to pull the doors apart. He planted one foot in the closet. Rising, Mandy backed up. The hanging clothes dangled overhead as Robbie grabbed hold of Mandy's hair.

She cried out, swatting his hand away. Her voice rose too high and he slapped her across the mouth, splitting her lip.

"I-I thought you were going to help me?" she stammered, tasting blood.

He sighed, releasing his grip so he could frown at her like she was a dumb child he didn't have the patience for. "Let's be real. Your little trick is bullshit. I can't do anything with it. *I'm* not gonna fuck a corpse. Maybe my dad could've snuck you out of the country or sold you off somewhere, but *I* don't have those connections. But you know what I got? Money, and lots of it, coming my way. All I gotta do is hold on, sit tight and wait, keep my nose clean."

She nodded, listening eagerly.

"But first things first — there are too many bodies around here. I can't call the authorities to deal with Dad until I tie up a few loose ends."

Bodies? Chaz and Mr. Pomerleau were back on the farm. The only dead body at the house was in the Pontiac's trunk. Then her eyes met Robbie's dull-eyed stare and she knew.

After she brought the others back (if that was even entirely possible), she would be next. She was the final loose end.

This time she didn't cower or wait or beg. She rammed the base of her palm into his nose, mashing the cartilage.

"Fucking bitch!" he spat.

Mandy shoved past him. She was out the door before he spun around, spewing more expletives. She had to get downstairs and find Mr. Pendleton's assistant. Women helping women. She would call the police and Mandy could go home, or at worst, to a jail cell, but one far away from Robbie.

The big, unfamiliar house disoriented her. She was turned around, and where she thought the stairs had been was wrong. She was further down the hall, deeper in the house. Robbie stepped out of his room, bearing his teeth. He spat a wad of blood onto the floor as he began stalking after her. With only one way to go, Mandy turned and ran — right into the office at the end of the hall.

She slammed the door in Robbie's face and locked him out. He roared, demanding she open up.

"No! Go away"

Robbie lowered his voice. "This is not your house. You're trespassing and I'm going to have you shot and killed. You're not leaving this place alive, *you stupid fucking corpse fucker!*"

The heavy door rattled in its frame, but held. He was blocked out for now, at least until the police broke it down (she doubted he would call them while Marisol's body decayed down below). Until the door was breached, she was alone in the office — which no longer enveloped her like a cozy, wood-paneled cabin.

She was alone with a dead man.

As the daughter of a funeral director, she felt bad that Mr. Pendleton was not being properly cared for. Though it wouldn't hurt him to stay there while his family grieved, there was no grieving in this house. Only scheming.

Mandy knelt down next to him. She held his hand and tried to think kind thoughts of him, though she didn't know him. That was for the best. Her first impression hadn't been great.

"I'm sorry," she said, as Robbie raged outside. Something heavy smashed against the door, then shattered on the floor. "I shouldn't have done that to your son. Shouldn't have brought him back. I didn't know he was like ... *that*. I should've just left him alone."

But at least she knew her "gift" hadn't been a fluke.

We've all got some weird trick we can do... What's yours?

Trevor's words never left her. She had so few memories of him since his death that she could only replay the same ones over and over. Even then, so many of them were fading away, disappearing with time. One day, she would lose him completely.

A trick, a gift, a curse — whatever it was, it was the only skill Mandy had. She never went to college or trade school. She was taught how to help run her father's business without receiving any professional training. Her time in the rest home had been for that only — rest. And since returning home, all she had done was keep her head down and get back to work.

She didn't have any people skills. Her tongue twisted when others tried talking to her — and that was if they didn't know she was the town monster who butchered the dead body of football hero Trevor Hardisty. She didn't know computers very well, or how to cook. She wasn't so good with animals and preferred to be alone.

Now, trapped in the office of a dead man, she wished she had learned how to throw a punch or fight.

But no. The only thing she knew how to do was bring a dead man back to life.

"I'm going to fucking kill you!"

Mandy didn't doubt that. Robbie never intended to help her. He only wanted to use her. And if she wasn't going to make his problems disappear, then she was no good to him, and he would rather see her die than lose his fortune.

Robbie had money and power and strength. He had his father's reputation to hide behind. He was a golden boy with friends who loved and believed in him.

Mandy had nothing but a curse.

Nothing but a curse that turned a dead man into a homicidal maniac, destroying everyone in his way. All Mandy had to do was step aside.

Locking her fingers between Mr. Pendleton's, she lifted her skirt and guided his hand between her legs.

CHAPTER 20

"*I'm going to fucking kill you!*"

Robbie hurled his body at the locked door. His rage made him invulnerable to pain. He scratched his fingernails down the hard wood, snapping two off. Pleading with the door to open, offering flesh and blood. But nothing and no one would open the door.

And that just made him even angrier.

He pounded his head against it, growling under his breath. As his jumbled thoughts lumped together to form somewhat of a plan, he was interrupted.

"Umm?" His dad's assistant, Gianna, tiptoed down the hall toward him. He glowered at her over his shoulder. "Oh my god. Did your little friend lock herself in there? With ... with *him?*"

"Can you open it?"

"I don't think so. Do you have a key?"

He slowly pushed back from the door, turning around to face this vapid, useless person. She gasped at the sight of his bloodied, broken nose, which he wiped on the back of his hand.

"If I had a key, Gianna, don't you think I would use it?"

Gianna giggled nervously, rolling her eyes at herself. "Oh my god, yeah. Yes. You would. So stupid..."

He held out his hand. "Will you help me open the door then?"

"Uh, sure. Yes, absolutely. But don't you think we should call an ambulance?"

"He's dead. There's not much else we can do."

"But—" She grimaced, an ugly expression on her otherwise stunning face. Robbie wanted to mash his mouth against her lips, forcing her to taste his blood. "—we can't just *leave him* in there."

"I know," he said. "That's why I need your help."

He moved his hand in front of her. *Take my hand.* She looked at it as she slowly placed her long, delicate fingers on his palm. He clamped around her like a Venus flytrap, pulling her in close.

She fought weakly, but there was nothing she could do. She was his now.

He pinned her to his side. His other hand gripped the back of her neck, guiding her toward the locked door. He wasn't going to beat his own head against the wood anymore, but that didn't mean Gianna couldn't assist with that.

He bashed her head against the door.

"No!" she cried. Her perfect nose bent, gushing blood. Her eyes turned inward, disappearing up inside her head. Robbie laughed. She looked like a fucking moron.

A few more bashes and she slumped down. He let her go. Her head wasn't nearly as mushy as Chaz's had been, but it wasn't holding up well as a battering ram. He let her body slide to the floor, leaving a bloody smear down the door, which remained intact.

"Fuck," he spat. Another loose end.

He was going to have to burn the house down. It would complicate his plans to collect his inheritance, but he was low on ideas and running out of options.

"Shit."

As he drummed his fingers against his lips, the door cracked open.

About fucking time.

But it wasn't Mandy the mousy-faced bitch who appeared. It was his dad.

Mr. Pendleton stepped forward. He was pale and sickly. One hand clutched his chest. His glassy eyes looked right past Robbie and only skimmed over Gianna's broken, bleeding body.

"Mmm," he rumbled.

Robbie wanted to grab his own shocked heart, but he was too stunned to move. Though he was no doctor, he was certain his old man had been dead. But heart attacks are tricky things — how could he be sure the man was dead without a heart monitor?

No, he was dead. He had to be. Gianna checked too. There's no way. This can't be possible—

Mandy.

He looked over his dad's shoulder as Mandy pried open a window and began to climb out. She looked back at them. At Robbie. Her eyes burned with hate.

The feeling was mutual.

"You fucking bitch," he grumbled, stomping toward her.

His dad's arm flew up, blocking his path. Robbie pressed forward, but his old man was strong. He refused to let Robbie pass.

Robbie forced his arm down, making another play to capture Mandy. But Mandy slipped out the window and disappeared into the night. She landed in the bushes below with a thud and a cry. He hoped the fall hurt like hell.

His dad hauled him out of the office and hurled him to the floor. He landed next to Gianna, slipping in her blood.

"It's not what it looks like," Robbie said. "Sh-sh-she tried to open the door and slipped and fell. You've seen her dumb fucking high heels. Accident waiting to happen."

Mr. Pendleton rumbled again. He grasped the collar of Robbie's shirt, pulling back a fist. Robbie held up his hands, crying out and turning away, pleading.

"Jesus Christ, Dad! Fuck! It's her fault! It's Mandy!"

The punch hit Robbie hard. Blood trickled from his lips and nose. He poked a loosened tooth with his tongue, drooling pinkish fluid down his shirt.

As his dad moved to strike him again, Robbie tried to pull his fist down. *"No! It was Mandy! She did this! She fucking did this to you!"*

Another punch. This one knocked Robbie's head back. He slunk backward. The dead weight of his body pulled his collar from his dad's fist. He hit the floor. Everything was spinning around him. When he looked up, his dad alternated between clutching his heart and grasping for Robbie's shirt.

Robbie pedaled backward, shaking his head. His dad stalked after him. "No!" Robbie shouted. "Go away! Fuck off!"

Then he brought his foot up and kicked his dad square in the chest. Right in the heart. Mr. Pendleton gasped and fell onto his ass with a grunt.

Breathing heavily, Robbie stared at his dad, who sat there in a daze. *Fuck*, he thought. *He* is *still alive. Fucking Mandy.* Then: *There goes my fucking inheritance.*

He got up. He spat out a glob of blood, walking over to his dad.

"Dad?" He held out his hand. He had to face facts. He had royally fucked up. His future fortune was at stake. Mandy had done what she had done, and he would make her pay for that, but now his dad had witnessed what she was capable of and together they could make her life a living hell.

How many men died suddenly without a will, leaving behind their families and fortunes? Mandy's weird body trick could solve so many succession problems. The Pendleton men could parade her around the world, getting rich off of her by giving wealthy men second chances.

So Robbie offered his hand to his dad. Together they would make this work. They may not be the epitome of father and son relations, but they could strike a balance in being business partners. All his dad had to do was take his hand.

Mr. Pendleton's glassy eyes studied the hand before him. And then he bit it.

CHAPTER 21

R obbie howled. He couldn't pull away. His dad chomped down on his flesh and bones, refusing to let go.

"Fucking son of bitch!" Robbie ripped his hand free. The tip of his middle finger remained pinched between his dad's teeth. Hugging his hand to his chest, he stumbled away.

He ran to the stairs, pausing at the landing to look back. His dad spat out the bit of finger and began a brisk, steady walk after his son.

No way in hell was Robbie sticking around. He dashed down the stairs. His ankles tripped over themselves and he bashed against the bannister. Catching himself, he rushed down the last steps and fell into the waiting arms of old security guard Henry.

"What's going on in here?" Henry asked, one hand hovering above his holstered gun and the other holding his radio. "I tried calling y'all, but no one answered, so— Oh, hi, Mr. Pendleton."

Robbie spun around. His dad was down the stairs already, grinning maniacally. Robbie ducked behind

Henry, pushing him toward the danger. It wasn't Robbie's job to deal with this shit, even if that shit was his dad.

Henry stumbled forward. "Hey, easy there," he warned Robbie. He turned to Mr. Pendleton, dropping his hand away from his gun. "Sorry to disturb you, sir. I just heard a lot of screaming. Having a game night? No, wait — hockey's on! Oh, boy, I'd love to know the score. I think our boys could make it to the playoffs."

Mr. Pendleton launched at Henry. Before the doddering fool could blink, Mr. Pendleton punched him. Henry's head rocked back, exposing his wrinkly throat. Mr. Pendleton went for the jugular. Blood burst out, splattering across Robbie's face.

The security guard flailed, sinking to the floor. He never drew his sidearm. He died with his boss (literally) chewing him out.

Robbie didn't blink. He ran to the kitchen, bypassing his dad gnawing and tearing at Henry's throat. He tripped on the edge of the sunken living room and flew toward the marble-topped island. He caught himself, checking behind.

His dad wiped blood from his face. Chunks of Henry's gore were lodged in his stained teeth. He was coming for Robbie next.

Shit, shit, shit! Robbie pulled open every drawer, but it had been so long since he had lived in the house. The cleaning lady must have reorganized everything because Robbie could not find the knives — only a junk drawer with plastic takeout cutlery. *Shit!* He was backed into a corner between the fridge and the electric range, above which dangled pots and pans. Robbie knocked his head against one.

Shit.

He grabbed the biggest cast iron frying pan. Flexing his fingers, he got into position — batter up! His dad just laughed.

He had always laughed at his son, no matter what Robbie tried or wanted to do. Robbie's hopes and dreams had all been a joke to the older man. He thought his son was a fool; hopeless, useless, worthless. Unwanted.

Gritting his teeth until a molar cracked, Robbie sneered. *"Come here."*

His dad dodged the first swing. He grabbed Robbie by the collar, slamming him against the counter. Caught in a violent embrace, Robbie whacked the pan against his dad's back. The man let go. Robbie shoved him back, far enough to swing again.

His dad took a step closer, blood oozing from his mouth. He let it spill on the floor before asking, "Oh, come on, son — don't you have a hug for your dear old dad...?"

Robbie swung. The pan connected with the side of his dad's face. Mr. Pendleton's jaw dislocated as his body swiveled around, trying to catch up. He spun out, slipping in the blood. He landed on his back and laid painfully still.

Robbie released a shaky breath. He reached down to check on him. "Dad—?"

Eyes wide open, his dad snapped at him, nipping at his fingers. Robbie shouted out, stumbling away. He raised the pan above his head and before his old man could stand on his own two feet, he drove the cookware down on his head, denting his skull.

Mr. Pendleton's eyes rolled up as he collapsed. Brains and blood leaked through his broken head. He groaned, grasping at Robbie's foot.

Robbie screamed. He struck him again and again. He didn't stop until the pan's handle became so bloody that it slipped from his hand and crashed to the floor. Robbie knelt next to the body and wailed.

He had killed his dad.

No. No. No — it wasn't me. I didn't do anything wrong. I was defending myself. He tried to kill me! He's older and bigger and stronger! And meaner! He was never a good dad. He was a piece of shit. He wanted me dead. He wasn't right. His heart... Yeah, his heart *killed him. That's right. It fucked him up. He came back wrong because of it. Just like Mandy said.*

Mandy! She did it! She used him. She *tried to kill me! She used my own fucking dad against me, that bitch! Fucking cunt!*

I'm gonna kill her!

He stood up. He left the kitchen. He strode out of the house, sniffing the air as if he could track her scent. He was the wolf and she was the prey. She couldn't have gotten far — the Pontiac was right where he had parked it, though the garage door was now open. The keys were in the ignition. *Stupid bitch.* She had missed her chance to escape and now he was going to hunt her down and kill her. He got behind the wheel and revved up the engine.

I'm coming for you, bitch. And I'm going to fucking destroy you.

He sped off down the long dirt road. It wasn't long before he found her, just beyond the guard station. The headlights reflected off her hair and skirt. She was running along the side of the road, just within the tree-line. She glanced back, slack-jawed and wide-eyed. He flashed the high beams, blinding her. Covering her face, she darted into the woods.

He pulled over and parked the car. When he got out, he took the keys with him. He didn't want her to circle back and steal the car. At this point, he would not put it past her. This time, he wasn't playing around. He was on the hunt.

He broke into a run.

I got you now.

CHAPTER 22

M andy froze under the glare of the headlights. Shadows shifted between the trees, and in an instant, nothing seemed real — excerpt for the rumble of an engine. She twisted around. The Pontiac's high beams burned into her eyeballs. Disoriented and blinded, she veered into the woods.

Branches snagged her clothes and hair, ripping out strands and taking scraps. She ran blindly, blinking fiercely to force her vision to return.

Her foot hit a clump of dirt and rock, and she barreled toward a fallen tree. She scrambled over, looking back but only seeing the *flashing, flashing, flashing* of the phantom headlights. She paused, held her breath, and listened.

Beyond the frantic pounding of her heart, she heard footsteps and panting. The woods around her shivered, forced to give way to the angry entity coming after her.

"Mandy!"

No time to sit around and listen. Mandy bolted over the tree. For the next several minutes, she ran. She dodged. Branches and dead leaves scratched her face. Something jabbed her eye. Tears leaked out as she kept going. She had never run so much in her life — and she was quickly losing steam.

"I know this place like the back of my *fucking* hand! I *will* find you!"

His voice sounded farther away. Had she lost him? She leaned against a tree and waited. Her pulse throbbed in her throat. She gulped for air. Maybe if she could hide under some leaves—

"Ah-ha!"

Hands caught her by the neck. Robbie stepped out of the shadows, huffing and puffing. Heat radiated off his body — but his hands were still terribly cold.

He throttled her against the tree, hitting the back of her head against the rough bark. He chuckled humor- lessly. "I don't know what pisses me off more: that you fucked my dad or that you made me work so hard to catch you."

"Where is he?" she wheezed, his thumbs pressing against her windpipe.

His bottom lip trembled. "Dead."

She sucked in a sharp breath. When she resurrected Mr. Pendleton, she had hoped he would attack Rob- bie. She never meant for him to die ... again. She just needed to buy some time to get away.

"Sorry," she croaked.

"Fuck your sorry!" he yelled. Exhaling, he un- clenched. "Fuck everything. He was an asshole, but he was still my fucking dad. You don't *do* that to some- one's family. It's fucked up. *You're* fucked up."

"I know," she muttered. "I'm sorry."

He wiped his lips, snorting back snot.

Mandy held onto the tree and thought about running. But he was too close and much too fast. She scanned the ground, hoping to see through the darkness and find a weapon — an abandoned knife, a large branch, a sharp twig — hell, even a rolled-up magazine. And while the flashing had faded, she couldn't see much in the dark.

Robbie stabbed a finger at her. "You wouldn't like this shit happening to *your* old man."

No, she agreed. She loved her father. He was innocent and he had suffered enough for her transgressions.

"But maybe that would make us square," he said, a gleam in his eye.

She shook her head, whispering, "No..."

He squeezed her shoulder. "You know what I did to Chaz? Oh, Mandy baby, it's gonna be *so much worse.* You're dad's gonna be buried in a goddamn soup can."

She kept shaking. "No, just leave him alone. This isn't about him."

Head bobbing, he pushed her through the woods. "Oh, yes it is. You killed my dad, so now I'm gonna kill yours."

"I didn't kill your dad," she argued, digging her heels in. "*You* did. Leave my father alone. He's never hurt anyone in his life."

"I don't care if your dad is Mother Theresa or Lady fucking Gaga. I'm going to make you pay for all this bullshit you put me through — starting with your dad."

She struck him with her elbow. Her bone hit his rib cage, sending an electric jolt of funny pain through her arm and nervous system. She folded over. Robbie took control. Though weak and exhausted, she still had some fight in her — but not enough to do more than make herself as heavy and obstinate as possible.

All the way back toward the glowing headlights and the exhaust sweeping across the road like fog, Robbie grumbled about how he was going to make her pay, arguing that it was *Mandy* who killed his father. It was *her* fault. *She* was responsible for all these deaths, and deep down inside, she felt responsible, though she hadn't swung the wrench that killed Chaz or dealt the killing blow to Mr. Pomerleau. Robbie's victims would still be alive if she had just left well enough alone.

If she hadn't discovered her gift.

Not a gift. A curse.

Robbie dragged her to the car and threw the door open. Before he forced her inside, he threw her against the hood and gave her a slap.

"Now listen up. No funny stuff. You're not gonna get away with shit. You try anything and I'll pull this car over and you can ride with my dear friend Marisol back there." He waved a hand in front of his nose. "My nose is fucked up, but I can tell she's getting pretty ripe."

She glanced at the trunk. He snapped his fingers in her face.

"And that's not all. If you do try something, I'm going to kill your old man *and* make you bring him back. You know why? So I can *fucking kill him again.* Got it?"

A wave of nausea washed over her. She nodded, not breaking eye contact. She wanted him to know she heard him loud and clear.

"Good. Get in."

He shoved her inside. She didn't bother with her seatbelt. She glanced at the door handle. He knocked on the glass, pointing at her. *Don't even think about it.*

Keeping her head down, she stared at her hands resting limply in her lap. She thought about her father, and though she hoped he wasn't home — maybe he had plans to go away on business that he never told her about? — she also knew Robbie would make her wait. They would wait together until her father returned.

Robbie marched around the front of the car, his body lit up by the headlights. He came around to the driver's side and got in. As he shut the door, he reached over and squeezed Mandy's thigh.

"Night's still young," he said. "We're gonna have a really good time tonight. Unforgettable."

They started driving. Robbie kept one hand on the wheel, the other gripped her leg. His nails dug in until small crescent blood moons formed in her flesh. They drove in dead silence, just the sound of the road noise enveloping them — and Mandy's pulse pounding in her ears.

She held her breath and held on.

They were getting closer to her house. She recognized the old town signage, two bullet holes in the sheet metal. They passed the spot where Robbie had driven her into the ditch. Her truck sunk into the soft mud and grass, waiting for a tow just beyond Mr. Pomerleau's barn.

Almost there. Home, sweet home.

She exhaled. Breathe in, breathe out. Everything was going to be okay. She closed her eyes. She thought about Trevor. She reminded herself that even though he was much stronger and faster, she had stopped him. And she could do it again.

Robbie let go of her leg. He craned his neck to look over his shoulder.

"What?" she asked, studying his face.

He looked like he had seen a ghost, or that he was trying to calculate the probability of seeing a ghost. Or that he was trying to convince himself that whatever he had seen, it had been a trick of the light.

He adjusted the rear view mirror. "Nothing," he muttered.

Mandy stared ahead too, matching his posture and focus. "Nothing" was exactly right. Except for the reflection in the windshield, obscured by the highway lines whipping past the car. A long ghostly arm reaching forward.

It was time.

Mandy grabbed the door handle and yanked it open. This time she didn't think. She didn't count all her bones before they broke. She threw herself out of the vehicle. Robbie shouted something after her, but the car sped on without her.

She hit the pavement. Her arm cracked. The blacktop scraped her exposed skin. She tried to roll but that was easier said than done. She wasn't a stuntwoman or some kind of super spy. She had only ever seen this maneuver in movies. The road chewed her up and left her alone and cold and hurt.

Groaning, she laid in the middle of the road, holding herself. She looked up at the sky. Stars twinkled behind the floating wisps of clouds. Red lights flashed.

Rubber tires screeched across the road, followed by rumbling, shocks absorbing a sudden dip into a grassy, wet ditch. Then a sudden crash, over as soon as it began, followed by a low, melancholy horn.

CHAPTER 23

B efore the crash, something shifted in the back seat. Robbie sensed it, but when he glanced back, he didn't see anything. Or at least, he didn't think he had seen anything. It had to have been a deer that trotted out onto the road after the car had passed.

"What?" Mandy asked.

"Nothing." He wanted to tell her to shut up and mind her own business, but then her door was open and she fell out like a rag doll. "What the fuck?!"

She was just gone, swallowed up by the night.

Bubbling up with renewed rage, Robbie hit the brakes. Two long arms grabbed him from the back seat. He checked the rearview mirror. It wasn't a deer, it wasn't a trick of the light, it wasn't all in his head.

It was Marisol. She was alive.

She snapped her mouth open like a vampire's. No fangs, only teeth — missing a few from their last encounter. She bit down on his shoulder. He lost control, swerving into the ditch as he tried to swat her away.

He laid on the brakes, but the car was going too fast to stop. He spun out of control and swerved off the road. He slid through the ditch, unable to find traction on the dewy grass. The car ploughed into a thick tree. *Crash!*

His butt lifted off the seat on impact. No seatbelt, no safety. His head broke through the windshield. The glass cracked, shattered, embraced him, sliced him. He flew out of the vehicle. His legs busted on the way out. The only thing that stopped him from hitting the tree face first was that his shoe caught on the steering wheel. His ankle bone dislocated when he plopped down on the hood.

He laid on his stomach for eternity. All he could do was blink and swallow. He listened for his heartbeat. Everything was the same as before — *he was alive* — except that he was a broken, sorry mess.

He looked around. A branch had gone through the windshield, narrowly missing where Robbie's head had been. But it did not miss Marisol. It stabbed through the headrest and impaled her.

He chuckled, in spite of a broken rib or two that fired pain throughout his torso. *Fucking bitch.*

Now he could deny killing her. She died in a car accident, that was all. They had decided to get over their past grievances and become friends. They went for a ride in the country and then she died in an unfortunate accident.

He wiped away the blood seeping into his eyes, still scheming, still imagining how this could all shake out for him. Chaz and the old farmer would be tricky to explain, but his dad— Well, that was a coincidence. A break-and-enter gone wrong while Robbie was badly hurt in the wreck.

What a tragedy! What a poor family! What a brave soldier!

Robbie smirked, resting his head on the car's hood. *Don't fall asleep, asshole*. He wriggled his aching arm down to his pocket. *Gotta call 911 first*.

He couldn't reach his phone. It had to have fallen out of his pocket at some point. It was likely laying on the floor or under the car seat. He shook his head at the futility of it. He couldn't even laugh.

He needed help.

Then he saw someone walking along the road. She cradled an arm against her body and hobbled along at a slow and steady pace. Her long, limp hair hung around her shoulders.

Fuck. It's Mandy.

"What do you want?" he asked.

She studied him silently from a safe distance.

He rolled his eyes — the only action that didn't hurt. "You gonna help me or what?" It didn't appear like she would, but she couldn't just leave him to die. She wasn't that kind of person. She hadn't done it before... "Come on. Just hand me my phone. That's all you gotta do."

She paused, as if considering it. Robbie let out a tiny exhale when she started limping down into the ditch. She took her time, her ankle bent awkwardly. *That's what you get for jumping out of a car, dumbass.*

When she finally made it down to the car, she didn't open the driver's side door, nor did she search for his phone. Robbie could barely crane his neck to see what she was doing — peering in at poor, dead Marisol.

"Come on..." Robbie groaned. He squirmed, trying to roll onto his side, but pain flared everywhere at once. He cried out. "Fuck, fuck, fuck—"

The trunk opened, then closed.

"No..." *No, you stupid bitch. My phone wasn't in the trunk. Jesus fucking Christ.*

Mandy shuffled back around to the front of the car. She stopped and stood beside him. She kept one arm close. The other held a hatchet, stolen from his dad's garage. It was sharp and glinted in the reflection of the headlights.

"No. No, no, no, no." His broken ribs protested his protestations. "You won, okay? It's over. Look at me — I'm fucked up. Just go. I'm done, all right?"

"No," she said softly. *"I fucked up."*

She raised the hatchet. Robbie screamed, and didn't stop until he passed out from blood loss. Then Mandy finished her work in silence, taking him apart piece by piece.

CHAPTER 24

It was nearly dawn by the time Mandy had finished correcting her mistake and continued home on foot. There weren't a lot of cars on this particular stretch of highway so no one noticed the girl in the blood-stained skirt. She maintained a slow and steady pace and watched for cars. She didn't need a lift; she just didn't want to get noticed, same as usual.

As she shambled home, she wondered how she was going to explain herself to her father. He would be worried sick. Anything would be better than the truth. The truth would send her back to the rest home, and she sure as hell didn't need the people in town talking about her or smearing her father's business again. None of this was about him. She had to keep him out of it, even if carrying the weight of such a secret slowly killed her.

But it was her secret, and burden, to bear. No one else's. She wasn't going to use it again, ever. If she could excise that part of herself and bury it deep underground, she would. Instead, she would have to learn to live with it, and hopefully, in time, forget it was ever there.

She would have to exercise better judgment if she ever dared to try it again.

And she wouldn't. Never again. Never ever.

She thought about Marisol's body in the trunk of the car. She felt badly that Marisol couldn't give her consent to participate in Mandy's scheme, but even in death, the girl champed at the bit for a second chance — *for revenge*. And wasn't that what Mandy's power was all about? Giving second chances?

She had done Robbie a kindness and he repaid her with violence. So she used her trick to help Marisol. And Robbie's dad too. She helped them teach that awful young man one hell of a harsh lesson, which was a simple one.

Don't fuck with the weird girl.

She had done what needed to be done, and she had corrected the mistakes that came out of it. And she too had learned a valuable lesson. Never again would she bring another person back from the dead.

A truck slowed down beside her, catching her off guard. She never meant to get lost in her thoughts. Now someone had seen her.

The driver rolled his window down. He was a strong-looking farmboy in a checkered shirt. He eyed her suspiciously. "Hey, you all right?" he asked.

Mandy looked up and down the long stretch of road. She was close to home. "I'm all right."

"Need a ride?"

She studied him. Something about his jaw line and the smile lines around his mouth reminded her of Trevor. With her good arm, she rubbed her eyes. "No."

"You don't look too good. Did something happen?"

She laughed until she gagged. The man looked concerned — and also ready to step on the gas and speed away from the deranged stranger.

"No, no," she said. "Just a car accident." She pointed her thumb back behind her. "Drove into the ditch. Just trying to get home."

"Oh, boy," he exclaimed, reaching over to pop open the passenger side door. "Well, let's get you home. I can call a tow truck if you like."

She looked inside. It was clean. Didn't appear to have any weapons or signs of past struggles. But getting in a car with another stranger didn't feel right, even though her ankle was killing her.

She stepped back and shook her head. "No, that's okay. I'm almost home."

"Are you sure? I don't mind—"

Her icy glare froze him. *"I just want to be alone."*

He shook his head, fumbling back over the console to shut the door. He mumbled something about helping people who wouldn't even help themselves. "Just trying to be nice... Why bother... Dumb bitch..." Then he sped off in a huff.

Mandy stood on the shoulder, watching him disappear down the road. Once he was out of sight, she continued on her way. Alone once more, she smiled into the orange sun spreading across the misty horizon. She could see her house up ahead.

And as she limped back to her old life, she promised she would never do it again. *Well... unless...* Unless someone was truly deserving of a second chance.

Or unless an impatient truck driver crashed into a tree and killed himself. Maybe she would. Maybe she would see what he could do for *her* this time.

After all, she was the one with the power.

It wasn't a trick. It wasn't a gift or a curse. It was just her. It was Mandy.

THE END

THANK YOU FOR READING!

From the deepest, darkest depths of my cold, dead heart, thank you for purchasing a copy of *Mandy*. If you've enjoyed yourself, please rate and review or tell a friend.

— S.S.

.

ABOUT THE AUTHOR

Retro horror author Stephanie Sparks writes stories reminiscent of classic '70s and '80s slasher and monster movies. She loves scream queens, final girls, and the masked maniacs who stalk them. Her books feature action, thrills, dark humor, and sarcasm. She prefers cats to people and when she's not lost in a paperback from hell or listening to 1980s movie soundtracks, she's daydreaming ideas for her next book or writing furiously.

The independent author of *The Stepchildren* and *Kill the Babysitter*, Stephanie Sparks is a member of the Horror Writers Association. She is working on her next novel.

Find her @stephazoidwrites (Instagram and Facebook) or at www.StephanieSparks.ca.

ALSO AVAILABLE

KILL THE BABYSITTER

Jane's first babysitting gig comes with a lot of rules, and after a hellish night, she breaks an important one: *Don't let the kids play with the Ouija board.* Now the mischievous spirit in the board wants to play a deadly new game: *Kill the Babysitter.* Jane must fight tooth and nail against a murderous horde of possessed children — and if she doesn't team up with her worst enemy, she may not survive the night.

········

SCREAM, QUEEN

1984... Beautiful, do-good student Becca has been nominated for the coveted role of queen of her town's Harvest Festival. But when she starts looking into its history, she discovers that each of the past queens died under mysterious circumstances — including her mom. There is something insidiously rotten about the festival, and if Becca can't escape her queenly duties, she will have to make the ultimate sacrifice.

············

THE STEPCHILDREN

Jamie had always suspected something was wrong with her stepfather. Burt wasn't just a man on the hunt for the perfect life — he was a fugitive family annihilator. Years after surviving his attack, Jamie and his other stepchildren come together in group therapy where they learn he has died in prison. Or has he? Turns out, even in death, daddy dearest has a few deadly surprises left for his wayward stepchildren.

See more at www.StephanieSparks.ca.

PREVIEW

THE STEPCHILDREN

"Call me Daddy," he said.

Fifteen-year-old Jamie Riley choked down the bland lump of cold, leftover wedding cake as she stared up at her stepfather, towering over her in his tan slacks and itchy sweater vest. It sure beat the obnoxiously white tuxedo he wore the day before. His muddy brown eyes bulged, magnified behind his thick-lensed glasses. Clutching a glass of warm milk, he rubbed at the milk mustache coating the bristles under his nose, not quite swiping it away.

The guy was a dork. From the day her mother sprang him on her — "Jamie, honey? I want you to meet someone" — to the moment he donned his wedding day best, Jamie rolled her eyes at his royal dorkiness.

At first, she paid him no mind, because he was just another guy in her mother's long list of losers, following in her father's footsteps. She figured he wouldn't last.

Burt was not like the others. He proposed to Christine after three months of dating, though Jamie suspected they had kept their coupling a secret for a few months before telling her. They tittered like teenagers when Christine gave him a tour of the house — *their house. Not his.*

He strutted around the place, eyeballing their family photos and critiquing Jamie's drawings, like he was some high-brow art critic. He straightened the frames on the wall and wiped dust away with his index finger. He prowled about, taking everything in. Looming over the mother and daughter in the living room, he was too tall for their house. Simply, he wasn't a good fit.

"I'm not calling him anything," Jamie vowed the night before the wedding. She toyed with her mother's veil. The wedding itself was lavish and unnecessary, but Christine never got a dream wedding with Jamie's dad. They married in a friend's backyard a month before Jamie was born.

"You don't have to call him anything," Christine conceded. "Just Burt. And if one day you want to call him 'Dad,' that's okay too."

Jamie had a dad already. Just not a very involved one. Tanner Riley was a deadbeat husband who walked out on them when Jamie was only eight. He came back from time to time to pay up his child support and take Jamie for soft-serve ice cream down the street. But he never had any fatherly wisdom to impart or love to give. He was more like a fun uncle, grinding up all his money and energy into getting his band off the ground.

When Tanner walked out on them, Christine uprooted her daughter. She convinced her parents to help her buy a house in the Port Coquitlam neighborhood of Mary Hill with its rolling hills, established trees, and unique 70s-era homes.

They lived seven happy years there before Burt wiped his loafers on their welcome mat. The house became his almost overnight.

Jamie set aside the piece of cake, swiped from the fridge. A late-night snack for a late-night study session. Her mother may have just gotten married, but that didn't make her mountain of homework go away.

"Uh, what?" she asked as Burt reached across her desk and snatched the fork from her hand. "Hey!"

He forked himself a big bite, cramming the dessert into his mouth. Crumbs spewed out, littering her textbooks. Then he gulped down his milk, wiping his mouth with his thumb and forefinger, pinky and ring finger curled around the fork. His gold wedding band flashed. All the while, a whiny wind whistled through his nose.

"Mmm, that's good!" Then he added, "I just stopped in to say goodnight."

She rolled her eyes. "Goodnight, Burt."

"We're family now," he said. "Call me Daddy."

"Don't think so," she mumbled. Scowling, she reached for her sketchpad, hidden under her bio notes, and began scribbling. She hoped he would get the hint and go away.

"It's a little late for that, Jelly Bean," he said, pushing his nickname on her.

"Don't call me that."

Her desk lamp cruelly cast his long shadow against her door, making him even more imposing. "Time for lights out."

Ugh. Eye roll. "It's *only* eleven. And Mom lets me stay up as late as I want."

"Well, your mother and I had a discussion about that, and we think you would do better in school if you got the proper amount of sleep. A solid eight hours always does wonders for me."

"I'm trying to do my homework."

"It looks like you're doodling."

She shot him a frosty look. "It's for art class."

"Oh, really?" He raised an eyebrow over his dated frames, snatching the book out from under her. Her pencil scratched the paper, leaving a dark, unwanted, and impossible-to-erase mark. Her picture was ruined. Burt frowned, turning it from side to side. "I can't even tell what this is." He knocked on her bio textbook. "I'd recommend hitting these books. Art is not your ... strong point."

His opinion didn't hold water with her. Not only was he a dork, but he was a boring, old real estate agent who liked bugs. He didn't have an artistic bone in his body and he wouldn't know good art if it walked up and bit his nose.

Yet, the criticism stung.

"Give it back," she demanded.

He tucked the pad under his arm. "It's time for bed."

"Give it *back.* "

Shadows grew longer, deeper on his face. The reflection on his lenses masked his dark eyes. *"I won't tell you again."*

Grumbling, she jumped up from her desk and slammed the chair against it, which rattled the mirror against the wall and shook the lamp. She stormed to her bed, pulled back the comforter, and plopped down, arms crossed. "There. Happy now?"

He pointed to the lamp. "You forgot to turn out the light."

She puckered her face. "I want it on."

"I said it was time for lights out. Turn. Off. The. Light."

"Back off," she muttered. She knew how the words sounded coming out of her mumbling mouth, but she would never actually swear at an adult. Her mother would lose her shit. But Burt didn't know her well enough, just as she didn't know anything about him. Yet.

But he didn't yell or run off to tell her mother. He took two swift steps to her desk, wrapped his fist around her lamp, and marched off with it. The cord stretched, knocking her papers and books to the floor. As he left her room, he gave it one good, hard yank. Darkness blanketed the room.

Unsettled, she couldn't see where he had gone — until his breath hit her cheek. "Don't you ever *fuck* with me," he snarled. "And from now on, you call me Daddy. We're family now, so you better start acting like it."

He dropped the sketchpad on her thighs with a slap.

Then he left, the lamp cord trailing behind him.

She clutched the pad to her chest. *Fucking psycho*, she thought, tears threatening to spill.

She didn't know the half of it.

··········

133

Want more?

Find *The Stepchildren* and more at the following:

Amazon
Barnes & Noble
Blackwell's
Booktopia
Kobo
Waterstones

Or scan the QR code to visit my Amazon Author page: